M000012632

goddess tithe

To Dave,
With best Christmas
wishes!
Anne Elizabeth
Stengl

Tales of Goldstone Wood

goddess tithe

TALES OF GOLDSTONE WOOD
—+·+—

ANNE ELISABETH STENGL

ROOGLEWOOD PRESS
Raleigh, NC

© 2013 by Anne Elisabeth Stengl

Published by Rooglewood Press
www.RooglewoodPress.com

Printed in the United States of America

All rights reserved. No part of this publication may be reproduced, stored in a retrieval system, or transmitted in any form or by any means—for example, electronic, photocopy, recording—without the prior written permission of the publisher. The only exception is brief quotations in printed reviews.

ISBN-13: 978-0-9894478-0-5

This is a work of fiction. Names, characters, incidents, and dialogues are products of the author's imagination and are not to be construed as real. Any resemblance to actual events or persons, living or dead, is entirely coincidental.

Book design by A.E. de Silva
Cover art by Phatpuppy, www.phatpuppyart.com
Interior illustrations by Anne Elisabeth Stengl

To Kyle,

for a great idea

DEVIL
IN THE
HOLD

S HE WILL ALWAYS CLAIM her tithe," the old man said. "Such is the law of this sea."

The boy sat cross-legged before the old man, tying knots as fast as his small fingers could fly. During the months of this, his first voyage to the western reaches of the great Continent, he had learned to tie more than twenty different knots under the old man's direction. As a little child on his mother's knee, the boy would never have believed so many knots existed.

But that was long ago. A lifetime, it seemed, since he kissed his mother goodbye; perhaps forever. Since then he had begun to learn the secret of knots, and his fingers had toughened until the rough fibers of the ship's ropes could no longer flay them to tear-blinking agony.

"When you have learned a hundred knots, then you will be a sailor," the old man had said. The boy believed him, because he was so old and so ugly that he must be very wise.

This was why the boy also believed the old man when he said, "Just you wait, young Munny. Captain knows the laws better than you or I ever will. He knows what she demands."

The boy—who was called Munny, though this was not the name his mother had given him—glanced uneasily over his shoulder toward the hatch that led, eventually, down to the *Kulap Kanya*'s deepest hold.

The hold where the devil lurked.

"Why," Munny asked, "does the Captain not give him over? We have been six days at sea, and still he is down there!" Munny shivered as he spoke, for the devil in the hold frightened him.

But the old man reached out and tapped him sharply on top of his head, hard enough that it hurt and brought the boy looking round again. "Do I hear you questioning the Captain, little sea-pup?"

"No, Tu Pich," Munny said, bobbing respectfully in an awkward seated bow, and focused once more upon his knots. He was practicing what the old man called the "Mother's Arms," and it was difficult enough for his small hands without the added pressure of the old man's scowl . . . or the dreadful chill of the hold's gaping mouth at his back.

He hunched over his work, fingers trembling, and was relieved when the old man, seated upon a large cask above him, leaned back at last and closed his eyes. The world was full of sounds: the creak of timbers, the shouts of sailors, the ever-present rumbling conversation of the wind and the sea. But somehow the old man could make the small sphere of existence around his wrinkled self seem a haven of calm. Glancing up at him every now and then, Munny felt calmer too, despite the lurking evil below deck.

"Never doubt the Captain, my boy," the old man said suddenly, his voice as creaky as the timbers themselves and equally as strong. "I've sailed with him two ten-cycles of years, and while I have withered and bent under the ocean's harsh caress, the Captain never has. He is as hale and hearty as he was the day I first saw him. He knows the laws of the sea. He will honor Risafeth when the time is right."

Even as the old man spoke, a sudden change in the air brought both him and the boy sitting upright and twisting their heads about. All those upon the deck did likewise, and all those running the tack lines, even up to the man in the lookout. As a well-tuned orchestra turns ever to its conductor, so the crew of the *Kulap Kanya* turned to Captain Sunan as he stepped from his cabin into the sun.

He was a tall, lean man with a face unweathered by the salty air he breathed. To the men of his command he was like an ancient hero out of legend come to life. How could it be that he was nothing more than the master of a merchant ship sailing between Lunthea Maly and the western trade city of Capaneus, back and forth with the regularity of the changing seasons? Such a man should not be bound to one ship, to one repeated voyage. Such a man should not deal with traders and the shore-hugging businessmen back home.

Such a man—or so Munny thought with a thrill in his thin young breast—should be fighting dragons and monsters and devils with his bare hands. He should consort with gods, goddesses, and Faerie queens.

But no. Instead, Captain Sunan commanded the *Kulap Kanya*, which not even Munny could pretend was the proudest merchant vessel on the seas.

Munny sat frozen over his work, watching as the Captain strode across the deck and mounted the stairway to the quarterdeck. There the quartermaster, Sur Agung, saluted smartly after the Noorhitamin fashion, his right fist pressed to his left shoulder.

A kick planted itself in Munny's thigh, causing him to drop his half-worked knot. Munny, startled, gave a cry and looked up into the face of Chuo-tuk, his nemesis.

"Get up, scrub-louse," Chuo-tuk said, speaking with the imperiousness of a prince, though he was only the boatswain's boy. However, he was bigger and older than Munny by six years, and if there was one rule Munny had learned in the months of his first voyage, it was to listen to anyone bigger than he.

Munny scrambled to his feet despite the old man's protests of "Leave him alone, Chuo-tuk. He's not bothering you."

Chuo-tuk ignored the old man and took Munny by the ear. "Get up there, quick-like," he said, with a vicious tug to emphasize his domination. "Find out what Captain is saying to old Agung."

Munny hastened to obey the moment his ear was released. He was often called to this sort of work, being small and light on his feet. It was easy enough for him to slip into shadows and crevices to overhear conversations the lower sailors were not meant to hear. It was a crime punishable by five lashes if he was caught. But Munny considered the possible threat of five lashes compared to the definite reality of a kicking from Chuo-tuk to be odds worth taking.

He climbed not the stairs themselves but the outside railing, clinging to the shadows just beneath the quarterdeck. The sea was calm that afternoon, the *Kulap Kanya* rising and settling as gently as a baby rocked in a cradle. For this, at least, Munny could be thankful, as he clutched the railing and craned his neck to hear what he might.

Sur Agung was speaking. "You'd have to ask Bahurn to know for certain. But I hear he's been swearing storm-bursts below about the 'large rat,' and I little doubt what his answer will be."

"Summon Tu Bahurn, if you please, Agung," said the Captain.

Bells were rung, orders were bellowed, and soon Bahurn the boatswain was scrambling up from the hold, swearing even now, "Dragon's teeth and tail and gizzard!" Munny pressed himself still further into the shadows of the stair, terribly frightened that Bahurn would spot him as he went past. But Bahurn was too busy swallowing his curses and pulling himself together to present a respectful front to notice one skulking cabin boy.

"What is the news on our . . . little problem?" the Captain asked when the boatswain had saluted.

"If I may respectfully contradict my captain, I wouldn't call him so 'little,' if I were you. He's found his way to the cheeses now, and we'll have no Beauclair blue-crust left to offer our masters in Dong Min or Lunthea Maly if he goes on unchecked."

From where Munny clung, he could just see the Captain's face. And—though he would never have told Chuo-tuk as much for fear of a disbelieving slap—he could have sworn he saw a smile tilt the corner of the Captain's stern mouth.

"We would not want to be without our prized Beauclair blue-crust come trade day in Dong Min, would we?"

"No indeed, Captain," said Bahurn.

"The time has come then," said the Captain. "Our hold-devil has become too much of a nuisance. Bring him to my cabin, will you?"

"With pleasure!"

Munny dropped quietly from the rail, backing into a dark recess even as Bahurn flew down the stairway, roaring, "Saknu! Chuo-tuk! I require your assistance in lower storage!"

So Chuo-tuk was called away, scrambling down to the lower hold before Munny could bring his report. Munny scurried back to the old man, who remained sitting upon the cask, gazing out to sea as if he was not at all interested. But Munny knew he was and hastily said, "They're bringing him up, Tu Pich! They're bringing up the stowaway at last!"

"Ah. This is good," said the old man. "Risafeth will have her due, and our voyage will be safe." He smiled then, displaying his three yellow teeth. "Did I not tell you the Captain would do what he must when the time was right?"

Munny did not answer. He could already hear the shouts and sounds of struggle deep down in the bowels of the ship. He stood a little behind the old man's cask, breathless as he waited.

Soon Bahurn and his two sturdy boys appeared through the hatch, dragging the brown foreign devil behind them.

SECRETS SPOKEN and HEARD

GROWING UP IN THE VAST trade city of Lunthea Maly, Munny had seen his fair share of foreigners, from the ghostly pale strangers of Parumvir to the dark-skins of Southlands. His mother had taught him that they were all people, as human as any man or woman to be found in the Noorhitam Empire. For the most part, Munny believed her. She was his mother, after all. Mothers have a way of knowing things.

But his uncle Mokhtar had told him that all foreigners were devils or, at the very least, possessed by devils. "Look at the size of their eyes," Uncle Mokhtar would say. "See how big they are? That's because the devils get in that way, leaving them malformed. And you can bet if devils got in, they're sure to get out as well, quick as lightning! Watch for the devils, boy. Watch for the big eyes."

Somehow, the more horrible an idea is, the easier it is to believe.

Munny had no trouble whatsoever believing Uncle Mokhtar's warning as he watched the stowaway dragged kicking and screaming up from lower storage. He babbled at great speed and volume in a language Munny did not know, and his eyes were as large and wide as two black coins, windows through which any number of devils might comfortably pour.

Munny ducked behind the old man who, by contrast, continued to sit as placidly as ever upon his cask, only turning his head slightly to watch the progress of the boatswain and his boys as they hauled the culprit sternward to the Captain's cabin.

One thing was certain: If the stowaway was devil-possessed, they were not dignified sorts of devils. Indeed, when the brown foreigner flung himself headlong upon the deck, trying to cling to the boards by his fingernails, Munny fought to suppress a nervous giggle.

Chuo-tuk and Saknu grabbed their prey by his ankles and dragged him, scraping and clawing, several paces. Then Bahurn, snarling, took hold of him by his collar and, little caring if he choked to death, heaved him to his feet. Saknu caught him by one arm, Bahurn by the other, and Chuo-tuk followed behind, aiming kicks at the stowaway's backside as they went.

Bahurn, having twisted the stowaway's arm to the point of breaking, rendering him temporarily immobile, let go with one hand long enough to knock at the Captain's door.

"Shall I bring him in, Captain?"

"Yes."

"He's a sullen one. Not trustworthy. Shall I bind him?"

"That will not be necessary."

So the stranger disappeared into the cabin. Munny heard the thud of kicks, the scream of foreign curses, and the growl of Bahurn's voice. "Stand in the presence of your betters."

"Hard to stand when being kicked," the old man muttered, surprising Munny. The boy looked but could not read the wrinkled face beside him. Had he mistaken the sound of compassion? Surely Tu Pich would not feel sorry for a stowaway! Not when he knew what was coming for him.

At a command from the Captain, the boatswain and his boys withdrew, shutting the cabin door. Munny gasped.

"They left him alone! Tu Pich, the Captain is alone with the devil! What will happen?"

"Hush," said the old man. "Westerners do not understand the ways of the waters beyond Chiara Bay. Perhaps the Captain wishes to inform him of his fate in private. Allow him some pride."

Munny, considering the display he had just witnessed, did not think the stowaway cared two straws for his pride. But he had no time to question further, for the old man pinched his arm suddenly. "Tu Bahurn wants us."

Sure enough, Bahurn beckoned violently to the old man and the boy from his place of guard before the Captain's door. Munny scrambled hastily forward, leaving the old man to creak his way down from his cask and hobble more slowly behind.

"You wanted me?" Munny asked, bowing to the boatswain. Chuo-tuk, standing at his master's side, smiled smugly as though Munny had bowed to him. The hateful ape. That was one act of subservience Munny flatly refused to grant Chuo-tuk, no matter the kickings.

Grinding his teeth, Munny said, "How may I serve you, Tu Bahurn?"

"Chuo-tuk, take him up to the quarterdeck," the boatswain said. He spoke quietly, as though afraid to be overheard.

The old man, having now arrived, frowned. "What do you intend, Master Boatswain?"

"Never you mind," Bahurn snapped. "You go up with the boy and do as Chuo-tuk tells you. Under my order. Quickly now."

Munny ducked away from Chuo-tuk's grasp and scurried up the stairway to the quarterdeck on his own. Chuo-tuk, also afraid of being overheard, could not even curse him, but was obliged to follow in his wake, the old man trailing behind last of all. Upon gaining the quarterdeck, however, Chuo-tuk took up a stout rope and said, "Come here, scrub-louse. Tu Bahurn's orders."

"What are you doing?" the old man asked, even as he dragged himself up the last few steps.

"I'm not doing anything," said Chuo-tuk, and handed the rope to the old man. "You are. Secure him well; then we'll lower him down the side. Tu Bahurn wants to know what the Captain intends, and we can hear nothing through the door."

"Dragon's teeth!" Munny squeaked, the words tasting strange in his mouth. His mother had never permitted him to curse by the Dragon; but after many months at sea, Munny couldn't help picking up a few sailor phrases. He glanced across the quarterdeck to where the quartermaster, Sur Agung, stood with his back pointedly to them, gazing out across the waves. After all, if Munny was caught, it would only be a lowly cabin boy who received the five lashes. Sur Agung couldn't be held accountable for every misdemeanor among the crew, now could he?

"We'll learn the Captain's will soon enough," the old man protested, though his fingers already flew as they twisted the rope into the shapes he willed. "He will honor the goddess."

"Tu Bahurn didn't send you up here to question his orders," Chuo-tuk said, and folded his arms.

So the old man secured Munny in a hastily-formed harness. He finished it with a special knot of his own, saying quietly, "No fear, my boy. Pich's Knot has never yet given way. Not when tied by Pich himself."

Munny nodded, his eyes solemn. Chuo-tuk took him by the shoulder and pushed him to the railing. Looking over, Munny could see the small window on the starboard side: a window to the Captain's cabin. It was open to the lovely breeze that stroked the *Kulap Kanya* that day.

Afraid that Chuo-tuk would fling him over if he did not move quickly, Munny scrambled up onto the railing and swung his skinny legs over. Had the sea been rougher, he would have bashed himself rather severely on the seasoned wood of the ship's hull. As it was, he scraped several knuckles and the top of one foot as they lowered him down to the window. Chuo-tuk and the old man held the rope, looping it several times around the rail for added security.

Even so, Munny did not feel secure. Sometimes, living aboard the *Kulap Kanya,* he could forget how very near the sea always was, just beneath his feet. Here, however, suspended over the water with nothing but Pich's Knot to protect him, he felt the presence of the swelling waves like a vast entity, a huge life.

And down below—deep down, beneath the white foam, beneath the reach of the Lordly Sun's rays, moving alongside the ship but ever in its shadow—lurked Risafeth herself.

Munny shuddered and froze in place, his shoulder pressed against the wooden slats. The window was near, but he must first let that image pass from his mind. If he let it stay, he would not be able to move again.

His lips began to murmur, beyond his will. Words formed, tremulous, stolen away by the swift sea breezes. This did not matter, for Munny heard his mother's voice in his head, whispering to him as he had heard it many nights when, as he wakened from a nightmare, she came to him and held him close, singing softly to his fears:

"Go to sleep, go to sleep,
My good boy, go to sleep.

Where did the songbird go?
Beyond the mountains of the sun.
Beyond the gardens of the moon.
Where did the Dara go?
Beyond the Final Water's waves
To sing before the mighty throne.

Go to sleep, go to sleep,
My good boy, go to sleep."

Munny breathed again, and the image of Risafeth swam from his mind and allowed his heart to still. Ignoring the hissed curses of Chuo-tuk above, he lowered himself the last few feet to the window and put his ear as near as he dared.

"Dragons eat it," he whispered.

For he heard the Captain's voice, clear and deep, and he

heard the devil-ridden stranger answering, nervous and trembling. But they spoke entirely in Westerner!

The only words Munny had learned in the Western tongue were "Hello," "Good bye," and "Where is the privy?" He wasn't entirely certain that these were even correct, for Chuo-tuk had taught him, and Chuo-tuk had a wicked sense of humor. For all Munny knew, he could proudly say his words to a Westerner and end up with his head knocked off. So he'd never dared to try.

Still, he strained his ears to listen in, hoping he might pick up something here and there. But all he heard were names. "Lunthea Maly." His home city. "Pen-Chan." The ruling people of Noorhitam.

Then he heard the stowaway speak a name that was very strange. It was a name Munny had heard spoken only a few times in his life, always in hushed whispers.

"Ay-Ibunda." The Hidden Temple.

Now here was a mystery! What could the brown-skinned foreigner know of the Hidden Temple? And why should he speak of it to the Captain? Munny's mother had told him never to say the name out loud, and his uncle had grown violent the only time Munny asked him about it. It was a furtive name of secrets and, Munny suspected, evil.

Surely now the Captain would give the order and hand the devil-man over to his fate!

Curious, Munny risked putting tentative fingers to the frame of the window and pulled himself closer to peer inside. He saw the stowaway, looking rather the worse for wear (Beauclair blue-crust did not settle well in a stomach unaccustomed to tossing waves) standing across from the Captain, who sat at his great desk, his arms resting upon the arms of his chair, as rigid as a stone king.

Just then, the Captain stood and crossed his cabin to loom over the foreigner. How great and tall and strong the Captain was, even more so by contrast with the rumpled stowaway.

Suddenly, the Captain's gaze flickered to the window. Munny gasped and let go his hold, swinging backwards with the movement of the ship and striking his shoulder hard. He started to climb, hand over hand, his skinny legs kicking at the hull, his heart racing. This would mean more than five lashes! Oh, much more indeed!

Would the Captain have him thrown into the sea along with the devil-man?

Galvanized by fear, Munny achieved the railing in moments, and the old man and Chuo-tuk pulled him over and onto the deck. "What did you hear? What did the Captain say?" Chuo-tuk demanded, even as the old man worked to undo the complicated Pich's Knot.

Munny shook his head. "They spoke Westerner. All Westerner. I didn't understand." He could hardly get the words out and could not bear to say that he had been seen. Perhaps if he did not mention it then he could somehow make it so that it hadn't happened.

"Useless maggot," Chuo-tuk snarled and hastened down the steps to where the boatswain waited at the Captain's door.

The old man, to Munny's surprise, stuck out his tongue at Chuo-tuk's retreating back. "What did he expect? Foreigners never learn our language. They haven't the mouths for it, poor fools. There. You're free."

The rope harness slid away, and Munny kicked it across the deck and leaped back from it as if it were a snake. A sudden commotion below indicated that the Captain had emerged once more. Munny went white and grabbed the old man's hand. "Tu Pich, what if—"

"Hush," said the old man, for even then they heard Bahurn's voice bellowing from below, "Pich! Pich, come here, and bring the boy."

"Oh! Oh, dragon's . . ." Munny gasped, but hadn't the wits to think of any appropriate draconian anatomy in that moment. Clutching the old man by both hand and arm, he allowed himself to be led to the stair, and they looked down to where the Captain waited below. Beside him stood the stowaway who was, oddly enough, neither bound nor pleading for mercy.

The old man took the steps slowly, and Munny made every pretense of helping him in order to avoid facing his fate any sooner than necessary. But at last they stood before the Captain, and Munny felt the Captain's gaze like heated brands upon his face.

"How may I serve you?" the old man asked, bowing respectfully as a sailor ought to his master. Munny hastily added a bow of his own, his heart thudding the beat of sacrificial drums.

The Captain addressed himself to the old man, though his eyes never left Munny's small face. "I have vowed to give safe passage to this man, this Leonard, as he calls himself. In return, he will serve among my crew and earn his keep. I entrust him to you, Pich. Find him some proper clothes and teach him the ways of a seaman's life. See that no harm comes to him."

A hush fell upon the *Kulap Kanya*. Even the ship herself went silent, her sails still, her timbers scarcely daring to creak.

But the thought rang as loud as a shout, echoing through that silence, echoing through every living mind.

The goddess! The tithe! She will demand her tithe!

"Do you hear me, Pich?" the Captain said.

The old man bowed again. "I will do as you command," he said. He beckoned to the stranger. "Come here, brown boy. Come with me."

So the devil wouldn't be cast into the waves. Nor Munny either, apparently. They were spared.

And they were doomed.

BOTH HONOR AND CURSE

AILORS SEEMED TO MELT into the walls and floorboards, leaving a clear passage from the deck down to the lower sleeping quarters. In a vessel the size of the *Kulap Kanya*, privacy was a commodity of which only to dream, never to hope. So it felt strange and eerily wrong to Munny that he followed Pich and the devil-man down hatchways and through narrow doors without once bumping into a fellow sailor coming the other way.

All of them had fled the company of the stowaway. And now they fled the old man and Munny as well.

I'm cursed, Munny thought, hanging back so that he would not tread in the devil-man's shadow. *I'm cursed along with him!*

Oh, what would his poor mother say? And Uncle Mokhtar . . .

he would never allow Munny to cross his threshold again if he knew! Not that Uncle Mokhtar wanted Munny across his threshold to begin with.

"*The sailor's boy*," Mokhtar called his nephew, and he said it with as much abhorrence as he could ever say, "*The devil's boy*."

Even the sleeping quarters were empty. Not a single off-duty sailor lay cocooned in his sheepskin hammock, stealing a few hours of much-needed sleep. The hammocks hung slack and empty, their occupants fled to who knew what dark corners of the ship.

The old man moved as if he saw none of this, though Munny knew he must be far more aware than he pretended. Could Tu Pich even be frightened? It was difficult to believe that anyone so old remembered the meaning of fear. He certainly didn't look frightened as he dug out his small satchel of belongings and rooted through it for an extra shirt and trousers.

The devil-man, by contrast, looked as though he expected to have his throat slit at any moment. The gentlest rise and fall of the hull sent him stumbling and grabbing empty hammocks for support, and his enormous eyes rolled with the effort to look into every corner at once.

Why would a devil-man be afraid? Munny wondered, hanging back and watching the proceedings from a safe distance. Could devils fear?

Even devils must dread the goddess.

"Here," said the old man, turning to the stowaway, his arms full of woolen garments. "Put these on."

The stowaway, not understanding what was being said, looked at the clothes, made a face, and shook his head. He said something in Westerner, something fast that sounded like a protest.

"Flying fish-sprites," the old man cursed, shaking his head. Then he too spoke in Westerner, haltingly but with a certain force. When he had finished, the stowaway grimaced and, however reluctantly, took the clothing. Muttering foreign curses, he moved around to the far side of the nearest hammock and began to remove his outer clothing.

Munny took the opportunity to slip up beside the old man. They did not speak but watched as the stowaway unfastened a once-fine linen shirt, which was now badly rumpled and dirty. Munny thought perhaps he had seen servants from the fine houses of Capaneus City wearing such shirts. Had the stowaway been a servant once, before he turned to devilry?

And then, much to Munny's surprise, a garment of brilliant colors all jumbled together in a haphazard manner fell out from the front of the stowaway's unbuttoned shirt and landed on the floorboards. Even in the dim light of the one swinging lamp, Munny could see that the fabric was very fine, brilliantly dyed, but completely mad somehow, like a dye-master's nightmare.

The stowaway quickly picked it up, folding it and tucking it under his arm awkwardly even as he continued to strip and pull on the old man's ill-fitting garments. When he had finished, he stuffed the brilliant shirt down the front of his new tunic, then tightened his belt an extra notch to be certain nothing fell out.

"What is he, Tu Pich?" Munny whispered to the old man as they watched this odd display.

"He is our responsibility," the old man replied. "That is all we need know."

"But Risafeth will—"

"Never mind what Risafeth will or won't," the old man said

and pinched Munny's arm to silence him. "Our Captain has entrusted the stowaway to us. It is an honor. Captain is a Pen-Chan, and yet he gave this work to me and to you, who are but Chhayans. It is an honor," he repeated, as though to convince himself.

The stowaway, finished with his costuming, pushed his way back between the hammocks and stood before the old man and the boy. He caught hold of two hammocks, one in each hand, and used them to steady himself. His dark skin was slightly green-cast, but somehow, despite everything, he flashed the two of them an enormous smile.

"Well," he said, "it looks like we're stuck with each other for the time being at least. I do hope your shirt isn't quite as, um, *occupied* as it feels. I suppose I won't get lonely on this voyage, heh heh. So what are your names?"

But of course Munny understood none of this. And he thought to himself, *We're all going to die.*

CLIMB
TO THE
SKY

THE FIRST TIME THE STOWAWAY tried to scrub the galley floor, he ended up being sick all over it, more than doubling Munny's work. The old man just laughed and tossed Munny an extra rag. Munny, however, decided it was an evil sign and glared daggers at the stowaway's back as he stumbled from the galley and out to the deck, there to hang pathetically over the railing until his innards stopped trying to become his outards. Back during his first, stomach-churning days as a cabin boy, Munny had been able to hold his own innards down, even when faced with the grime and stench and rotted leftovers to be found littering the galley floor. Uncle Mokhtar would surely have declared his iron constitution a sign of his "natural-birth." But his mother, Munny knew, would have been proud.

What a limp, nectar-sipping butterfly the stowaway was!

In due course, the brown young man (looking more green than brown) slumped his way back to Munny's side and collapsed on his knees beside him. "Sorry about that. The smell, you know. Never liked the smell of sardines, and rotted sardines don't tickle my fancy much either. Did you already clear it all up? Good fellow; what a champion. I hope I can do the same for you someday . . . well, rather, not so much. Lumé love me, I hope never to see even a crumb of Beauclair blue-crust the rest of my born days!"

Munny glared at the devil-man, his small face managing to contain a whole world of disgust. But the stowaway didn't seem to notice and went on talking to himself even as he ineffectually ran a dirty rag over the section of flooring Munny had already scrubbed.

Munny turned to the old man. "Why does he keep chattering like an idiot bird?"

The old man laughed again. He sat on a stool with his arms crossed, enjoying one of the few advantages that old age brought his hard, sea-seasoned life: the opportunity to direct those younger than he and supervise them as they worked. "He's frightened. He thinks if he talks fast enough, he'll talk away his fear."

This sounded indescribably foolish. Munny glared at the stowaway again. Now the great idiot was wiping too near the brick-wrapped stove without looking where he went. He bumped right into the fire-warmed bricks, smacking his head hard. "Iubdan's *beard!*" he shouted, and the smell of burnt hair filled the small room. The stowaway's eyes went wide, and his face paled. "Iubdan's beard and . . . ugh . . . ."

The next moment he was staggering out the door again, making for the rail with all speed.

Munny watched this exhibition with enormous loathing. Shaking his head, he muttered, "Why doesn't Captain do what he should? Why doesn't he—"

He didn't realize how loud his voice was until he felt the back of the old man's hand on the side of his head.

"I'll not hear you mutter ill of the Captain," the old man said, leaning back and shaking his hand, which was not as sturdy as it had once been. "I'll not even have you thinking it. He'll do what he must at the right time. You'll see. You'll see."

So Munny swallowed his ire and focused instead on the task at hand. Scrub up, scrub down. Scrape the leavings, the rot, and the refuse into a pile. Scoop it with his own two hands into the pail. When the pail was full, haul it to the rail and feed its contents to the fish. Feed the fish and don't look into the waves, don't look beneath the foam.

Don't see the shadow of the goddess, following, following. Ever following.

The stowaway sidled up to Munny at the rail, wiping his mouth and wobbling a little. "Sorry about that, my friend," he said, smiling wryly even in the face of Munny's highly visible dislike. "I'll get the better of it eventually, I'm sure. I've never been to sea before."

Somehow it felt appropriate that the devil-man would jabber without meaning, so Munny didn't bother trying to understand. Swinging his bucket just hard enough when he turned that it grazed the stowaway's leg, Munny made his way back to the galley. The old man met both of them at the door.

"Good enough in there. Cook's next meal won't kill us, at

least. It's time you practiced your knots again, boy."

Munny sighed. After hours of bending, scraping, scooping, and pouring, he had hoped the old man would send him to his hammock for a rest. But he perked up when the old man said, "I think it's time you started to learn Pich's Knot. What do you say to that?"

"Yes, Tu Pich!" Munny said, delighted, his tiredness suddenly melting away. He had not thought the old man would trust him with this great secret for . . . well, years at least! Possibly never! After all, he had only just mastered his twenty-first knot, and he had a long way to go before reaching the hundredth knot that would make him a true sailor. Of such an honor he had never dared dream, to be taught the secret of Pich's Knot by Pich himself!

But Munny's excitement died a quick and irksome death when the stowaway fell into step behind them, following them from the galleys to a quiet place amidships where the great casks of Milden's Vineyard were lashed down and covered in canvas for safekeeping. Normally, casks such as these would be stored below, but the *Kulap Kanya* had stocked up on a much finer collection of Baie d'Où reds that would fetch a better price when at last they reached Lunthea Maly. So Milden's Vineyard was relegated to the deck.

The old man took a seat on the cask that had become his accustomed throne for these knotting tutorials. And Munny sat cross-legged at his feet and scowled at the stowaway, who sat cross-legged opposite him. "Does he have to be here?" Munny demanded sourly.

"Yes," said the old man, and no more. He did not need to explain. The shield of solitude that followed the unlikely threesome about the various decks of the vessel was answer enough. The other sailors refused any contact whatsoever with the stowaway and maintained their distance from the old man, the boy, and the devil. Munny could not guess what mischief might befall his unlucky companion should he wander far from Pich's watchful eye, Captain's orders notwithstanding.

The old man produced one length of rope and then another. These were not quite as large as the ropes Munny would someday attempt to work with, but they were better for learning the rudiments. "You know a basic hitch by now," the old man said.

Munny nodded. He glanced across at his dark companion, who was watching both him and the old man with interested but uncomprehending eyes. Were the devils inside him concerned with learning this secret too? And the old man, would he, without so much as a shrug, share his great gift with a devil-ridden foreigner?

Munny sank into a sulk so deep that he could scarcely listen to the old man's instructions. Indeed, anyone watching the trio would have assumed the stowaway was the student, so intently did he watch Pich's hands fly. But it was to the boy the old man spoke, and it was the boy who at last took the rope and tried to mimic his master's movements.

He knew how a basic hitch knot worked, and he'd learned the principles of Double Hitches and Cradle Hitches as well. But when he tried to make his fingers work the magic the old man made look so easy, they stumbled and dropped lengths of rope when they should have gathered them in, and gathered others when they should have dropped them.

At last he held up something that he thought *looked*, at least, very like what the old man had showed him. But the old man reached out and, with a simple tug, brought the whole thing flopping down across Munny's knees.

"I think," the old man said, "that you'd best keep to the Cradle Hitch for now. Until you're better able to pay heed to my instruction."

Munny scowled at the mess in his lap and, when he heard a laugh, scowled still more darkly at the stowaway across from him. But it wasn't the stowaway who mocked him.

"Flutter-fingers," Chuo-tuk said from where he stood just behind the stowaway, watching all with a superior expression. As though he knew anything about knots himself, the stupid Pen-Chan peacock! Munny felt his blood beginning to boil, and he would have liked to fling his ropes in Chuo-tuk's objectionable face. But to do so would mean a kicking, and the old man would not move to prevent it; not if Munny asked for it so blatantly.

"Make yourself useful, if you can, and get aloft," Chuo-tuk said, stepping around the stowaway to stand over Munny. "You're taking my place in the lookout."

"It's not my turn," Munny snarled, refusing to meet Chuo-tuk's gaze. "Do your own watch."

He gasped then as Chuo-tuk's sharp kick connected with his knee, knocking his leg askew. "What did you say to me?" Chuo-tuk demanded. "Eh? Want to say it again?" He drew back his foot for another kick.

But it never landed. The stowaway caught his ankle.

"Oi! If you like kicking someone smaller than you, kick me, why don't you?"

Startled as much by the foreign stream of talk as by the grab itself, Chuo-tuk unbalanced and landed with a great smash of his dignity upon the deck. The stowaway let go and got to his feet, his fists clenched as though prepared for a fight. Though he was older than Chuo-tuk by several years, he was smaller, wiry-limbed against Chuo-tuk's sailor's bulk. But he put up his fists and braced himself. "Come on!" he said. "Kick me!"

Chuo-tuk looked the stowaway up and down. But he made no move to fight, merely pushed himself up and backed away, his hands defensively out before him. "Debtor! Curse!" he hissed. Then he shot a furious look down at Munny, who sat watching all with his mouth agape. "So you'll have devils fight your battles for you? That won't do you much good when Risafeth comes to claim her dues!"

Munny said nothing. He stared from the stowaway to Chuo-tuk and back again.

Chuo-tuk rubbed his shoulder where he had struck it in his fall. "Tu Bahurn's orders, scrub-louse. You're to take my watch, and you're to take the devil-man with you. If you want to question Bahurn, be my guest! He'll make you bleed if he likes and send you aloft afterwards."

With that and a last sputtered curse at the stowaway, Chuo-tuk beat a retreat, scurrying to the forecastle and avoiding the looks of the sailors who watched him go.

"Well," said the old man, picking up Munny's rope and quietly beginning to tie it, "a foreigner is never short on surprises, is he?" Then he addressed himself to the stowaway, speaking in uncertain Westerner. "Do not fight boy, erh, his fights. He must fight or give . . . own choice. His honor."

His words were confused—his grasp of Westerner had never been strong—but he gazed at the stowaway with his bright black eyes, strangely clear for his age. "Honor," he repeated.

The stowaway shrugged. "I don't like a bully," he said.

The old man studied the stowaway's face, the boyish features as yet unhardened by age or by sea. He saw things there that others could not, and he grunted softly to himself.

Then he bent over suddenly and pinched Munny's ear. "You'd best obey Tu Bahurn, or it will be the worse for you."

"Must I take the devil-man?" Munny asked. His heart was thudding madly with a wide range of emotions, the primary one being fury. Fury at Chuo-tuk, perhaps, and at the stowaway. And maybe a little at himself.

"He is called Leonard," said the old man. "Learn it." With that, he closed his eyes, signaling the end of his part in the conversation. Even with his eyes closed, he continued to work the knot.

Munny got to his feet, uncertain whether or not to scowl, quite certain he wanted to cry, and hating himself for the desire. He was not a baby anymore. He could not run home to mother with scrapes and bruises, weeping, "*Why do they call me 'fish-spawn'? Why do they call me ill-born? Why do they throw things at me, Mother?*"

And he could not seek her comforting caress, her warm arms, and her soft voice saying, "*They are foolish and they are young. They don't know what they do. Pity them, my son, and do not hate them.*" Never again would he hear her call him by his true name—not Munny, but the name she had given him at his birth.

Those days were long past.

He would not cry anymore.

Clenching his jaw until it pained him, Munny beckoned to the stowaway, who glanced uncertainly at the old man. The old man, without opening his eyes, motioned with his hand for the stowaway to follow Munny.

The *Kulap Kanya* boasted three masts, the tallest in the center. These in turn boasted rigid battened sails spread against the sky like the wings of an enormous bird. On a day like this, when the wind was keen, the *Kulap Kanya* made great time, and men were constantly set to guard the tack line, running the rigging to keep the ship on course.

The center mast was crowned at its very top with a lookout's perch. The first few times Munny had made the climb, he had found it a harrowing journey and had been thankful enough for the securing line to which Tu Pich tied him to keep him safe.

Now, as he led the stowaway to the mast, Munny could feel the tension mounting in the strange man's body, emanating off his very spirit. Maybe the devils inside him didn't care for heights. Were devils bothered by such things as heights or depths?

The previous lookout was just descending when Munny and the stowaway arrived. The ruddy-faced sailor took one look at the stowaway, ducked his head, and moved on without a word, leaving the securing line dangling. Munny grabbed it and turned to the stowaway, motioning him to come forward.

"Oh, Lumé love us," the stowaway muttered. "You *are* expecting me to climb it. Lumé, Hymlumé, and all the starry host!"

"Come here, devil—" Munny stopped. The old man had told him to use the devil-man's name, and Munny never countered one of the old man's commands. "Come here, Lhe-nad," he said, uncomfortable with the strange sound of the word. "Come here, and I will secure you."

"Um. I don't know what you're saying. How about I just stand back and watch, as it were?"

But Munny caught the devil-man by the arm and began to

secure him with a Cradle Hitch. It wasn't as good as Pich's Knot, but it would do. It was all Munny himself had had on his first climb to the lookout.

Up on the forecastle, Tu Bahurn watched them as Chuo-tuk, standing near, gave his report. Munny glanced up at them . . . and suddenly his fingers paused in their work.

He could see the look on Tu Bahurn's face.

Bahurn would never dare to defy the Captain's express command. It would be treasonous to offer violence to a man the Captain had declared under the *Kulap Kanya*'s protection.

But accidents happened at sea. Especially under brisk winds.

Munny saw the look on Tu Bahurn's face and knew suddenly what he was expected to do. For a moment he stood frozen, the Cradle Hitch unfinished. The creak of the battens and the murmur of wind in the oiled cloth sails filled his ears.

Then he set his jaw and finished the knot. He pointed to the lookout perch and saw the stowaway's eyes cross as they rose up to that awful height and came back down again.

"Come," Munny said, and started for the mast. Grasping the climb ropes and placing his toes in the first of the footholds, he began his ascent. But the stowaway caught him by the shirt from behind.

"Wait! Aren't you going to tie yourself on? Where is your rope?"

Munny shook the stowaway's hand off. "Climb," he said, mistaking the strange words for yet another protest. Then he set to his own business, concentrating on the ascent before him.

He did not use the secure line now. He hadn't for several months, not since surviving his first Big Storm. During the long hours of that dark, endless night, he had feared for his life. But when dawn broke and the rain cleared and the damage was fixable and no hands were lost then Munny had decided something and vowed it with a certainty that he knew he could never break.

He would survive to reach Lunthea Maly again. It didn't matter what happened in the months intervening, he would survive. He would return home from this, his first voyage, and he would go to his mother's side. He would bring her the white peonies.

He knew now with utmost conviction, as he climbed the central mast and felt the tug of wind on his small frame, that nothing the wild ocean could throw at him would stay him in his course. Indeed, the only one who could stop him now was the goddess herself.

But she would have her tithe.

Munny heard the stowaway muttering and trying to talk away his fears as he climbed behind. Many times he heard the strange man bite out what could only be a curse. When he looked under his arm, he as often found the stowaway frozen with his arms wrapped around the mast as he found him climbing. Munny showed him how to secure his line on certain hooks in the mast as he climbed. Then he scrambled on ahead and soon pulled himself up into the lookout box.

He breathed the clearest of all ocean air up here and felt the wild thrill that seagulls must enjoy and albatrosses revel in. The rollicking of the waves felt so much wilder from this vantage, heady and huge and breathtaking. Somehow, though he was now many feet above the water, he felt closer to it than he did when he walked even the lowest decks of the *Kulap Kanya*'s hold.

I was born for the sea, Munny thought, and he recalled the cruel gibes of the alley children in the street back home. *Fish-*

spawn, he thought, and smiled. Maybe it was true after all. And maybe it was good.

Then he thought, *Where is she?*

At once he wished he could kill the thought and pretend it had never happened. But it was too late. He turned and, clutching the box rail, looked about, before, aft, to either side. In the great distance to the north, he could just see the hazy mound of the Continent. Gazing east, he could not as yet pretend to see the shores of Noorhitam, no matter how he might wish to.

To the west, behind them . . . behind them . . . Did she follow?

"Iubdan's beard and razor!"

Munny looked over the railing and found that the stowaway had managed to get himself up as far as the box. He was now attempting to catch hold of the floor and rails in order to hoist himself inside. A difficult feat when his hands shook like flags on a parade day.

Taking pity on him, Munny knelt and took hold of his wrist. "Come on, Lhe-nad," he said, pulling.

The stowaway managed to get one elbow up. His legs were now kicking into the empty void. Whispering what might be prayers, he stretched out his hand and reached for the railing.

Just as he did so, the ship gave an unexpected dive. It shouldn't have happened in that sea, under that wind, with the sails angled as they were. It shouldn't have happened, and yet it did. The whole lookout tilted, and Munny let go his hold on the stowaway to brace himself.

And the stowaway, with a strangled cry, plunged.

The world stopped.

Even the ship went still, poised for an eternity in that dive.

Tu Bahurn's face flashed before Munny's eyes, and everything his face had said.

Don't secure the line.

Give the goddess what she asks.

———

"Dragon's teeth, dragon's teeth, dragon's teeth!"

The world moved again. The ship recovered from her dive and leveled once more, progressing smoothly under a steady wind.

Munny, his heart in his throat, looked over the rail and saw the stowaway hanging a few yards below, swinging close to the mast and trying to catch hold.

The Cradle Hitch may not be as good as Pich's Knot. But it held true.

"You're alive! You're alive, devil-man!" Munny cried.

He realized, much to his astonishment, that he was glad.

THE STARS WHO FELL

"**B**AD LUCK," whispered Odi to his fellow rigger, Danung. Munny felt the blunt of Odi's elbow in his shoulder as the big sailor shuffled past.

"Cramped in here, isn't it?" said Leonard, rubbing his own shoulder where it had been likewise jostled. Then he shrugged and turned back to his bowl of dried fish, rice, and shriveled peas, tucking in as though it was the finest meal he had ever eaten. "I never thought I'd be so happy just to be *able* to eat!" he said around a mouthful. "Someday I'll write a song in honor of this very dish, and I'll sing it in the courts of kings."

Munny, by contrast, found every bite turning to ashes in his mouth. When he dared glance up, he caught Chuo-tuk across the room just turning his face away, his expression dark beneath the swinging lantern hung in the center of the room. Munny looked from him to Saknu, and saw the same turning away. So it was with every face Munny sought out. None of them would look at him or at his companion.

But Munny thought he could feel their very shadows watching him.

He had failed. He had been given the chance—however conveniently at Tu Bahurn's orders—to offer unto Risafeth what she demanded. And he had failed to honor her.

He had failed to honor the tithe.

Bad luck . . . .

Odi the rigger's voice rang in his ear. Perhaps he had meant nothing by the comment and it was only chance that his elbow had connected so sharply with both Munny and the stowaway. Space was cramped in the mess room attached to the galley.

Munny tried another mouthful, rolling it around on his tongue.

Risafeth knew her rights. She would claim them one way or another.

But Captain knows, Munny told himself, pushing the mouthful down his dry throat. *He will do what is right before it's too late.*

With that thought, he glanced to his side where Leonard scraped his bowl clean. Leonard caught his gaze and winked cheerfully, oblivious as always. Munny frowned. This voyage was becoming far more complicated than he had ever expected.

Bad luck . . . .

But surely it was good luck to honor the Captain's wishes! Surely it was good luck to save a man's life!

"Of course it is," the old man said half an hour later when he and Munny stood at the port rails, a yard or two upwind of Leonard, who was losing his supper into the waves. "It's always good luck when your own knot saves a life. Anyone who tells you otherwise is no true man of the sea."

"What about the goddess?" whispered Munny. Though he strained his eyes, this late in the evening he could not see the Continent to the north. They were alone on an enormous black ocean stretching forever on all sides. An ocean teeming with power Munny could not begin to comprehend.

"Today was not her day," said the old man firmly.

"She will be angry."

"Today was not her day," the old man repeated, and he lifted his own gaze from the waves to the sky. "How full are the moon's gardens tonight! The Dara dance overhead. Look at them, boy. Look at them and think upon their song. Risafeth is not the only force to which we are subject. The voice of vengeance is not the only voice to which we must listen."

Munny tilted his face heavenward, from the black expanse of ocean to the black expanse of space. The moon herself was not visible, but her children shone all the brighter, as though to make up for her absence. Not a cloud marred his view of the great gardens of the sky, where the Dara moved in their intricate dances, singing as they guided sailors across the waves.

On such a night, when all was still, Munny could almost believe he heard their songs with his own ears. He wished, very briefly, that he might climb up and take his place in the lookout. There, perhaps, he would be close enough. There, perhaps, he would hear the Dara sing, unimpeded by his own mortality.

Unimpeded by the retching sounds of the miserable Leonard, who was no longer so delighted with his supper as he had been.

"What do they sing, Tu Pich?" Munny asked.

"Many things," said the old man. "They sing of the past and of the present, which are all the same to them. They sing of the future, for which they long. They sing prophecies of heroes and monsters. And they sing of the promise given their mother."

At this Munny turned, surprised. He had heard many stories about the Dara during his voyage, almost as many stories as he had heard about Risafeth herself. But this was one he did not know. "A promise for their mother? What promise was that?"

"The promise that her lost children would return to her one day," said the old man, and his small black eyes seemed suddenly full of a hundred stars dancing in their depths. "The stars who did not fall will ever sing for the stars who did. They sing for their return."

He said no more but lapsed into a deep, impenetrable silence. Munny lifted his own gaze, which could not hold so many stars, and studied the patterns of the great dance above him.

A promise to their mother. A promise for the lost children to return.

Suddenly he felt as though his ears opened, receiving a sound and a song he did not know. The words fell upon him from above, rich and deep and sad.

"Beyond the Final Water falling,
The Songs of Spheres recalling,
When you hear my voice across the changing sea
Won't you return to me?"

Munny, his eyes filled with the first tears he had known since after his first Big Storm, vowed in his heart: *I will return. And I will kiss you again. Or I will lay the white peonies upon your grave.*

The singing stopped. Only then did Munny realize that it had been a mortal's voice he heard and not the voices of the Dara high above. The old man remained as stone, staring out into the night, but Munny whirled about, confused and curious.

To his surprise, and a little to his horror, he saw the Captain standing above them on the quarterdeck, also leaning on the stern rails, also gazing out at the sky. Munny could not see his face, for there was no moonlight to illuminate it nor any lanterns near enough. But he knew the form of his Captain as he would know the form of any hero stepped suddenly out of myth and into the real world.

And he trembled to realize what he had heard from this man who seemed to him too great and too terrible to feel real emotion. He had heard heartache.

"I take it back."

Munny startled and turned to find the stowaway making his way toward them, clutching the rail and wiping his mouth on his sleeve.

"I take it all back. I will never, and I do mean *never,* write any lyrics in honor of fish and peas. There are some songs not meant to be sung, and that, I am quite convinced, is one of them."

The old man held still for a moment more, unwilling to break his gaze with the Dara. Then he turned to Leonard and sighed heavily. "You talk too much," he said, and stumped away across the deck. The stowaway, with a baffled shake of his head and a bit of a smile, fell into place behind.

Munny followed as well. But before he went, he glanced up to the quarterdeck.

The Captain was gone as though he had never been.

DEATH
ON THE
WATER

ONE NICE THING ABOUT GODDESSES, Munny considered three days later while he and Leonard broke their backs on the quarterdeck, scraping away accumulated grime, was their tendency to stay in the realm of stories and speculation, rarely bothering to make their way into the real world to work their divine havoc.

Indeed, as time went on and the *Kulap Kanya* enjoyed fair winds and smooth seas, Munny began to wonder if perhaps Risafeth herself existed solely in the realm of myth and wasn't precisely *real* at all.

Not that he would dare voice such blasphemy in the old man's hearing. He liked his ears too well.

Besides, the more time he spent with the stowaway, the more Munny thought he probably wasn't devil-ridden. Uncle Mokhtar didn't know everything, after all.

Leonard had finally adjusted enough to the roll of the sea that he worked more often than he dangled over the railing. He even seemed to enjoy himself sometimes. "Salt, grime, sickness, bruised knees, the whole lot . . . this still beats kennel work for the duke any day!" he declared many times.

Though Munny didn't understand him, he saw the smile, and he thought it was friendly.

I'm glad my knot held, Munny told himself. *I don't care what the others think or say. I'm glad my knot held, glad that I tied it true.*

"You! Scrubber boy."

Munny startled at the voice of the quartermaster and looked up into Sur Agung's face. The quartermaster looked much older than the Captain, his steel grey hair pulled back from his forehead in a long, thin braid, and his skin so lined that his eyes nearly disappeared. But he was still strong and upright, with sinewy limbs that bespoke his years of hard seamanship.

He had never before bothered to look Munny's way. But now he stood over him, frowning. Something about his stance suggested he was trying to pretend that Leonard, who worked near Munny, did not exist.

"The Captain has called for you. He requires your services in his cabin."

"Me?" Munny gasped, sitting up and clutching his scrub brush in both blistered hands. "But Tu Niwut is—"

"Niwut is indisposed and cannot serve the Captain today." Sur Agung's lip curled as he looked Munny up and down. "Clean yourself up; put on a fresh shirt. Go on."

Sur Agung was not cruel—not like Tu Bahurn, still less like Chuo-tuk. But he was a hard man who demanded obedience, and Munny dared not hesitate, no matter how the blood pounded in his throat and temples. He dropped his brush and left Leonard on the quarterdeck under Tu Pich's supervision.

Does the Captain remember? Munny wondered as he climbed down to the sleeping cabin and dug out his one change of clothes. He had been issued a cabin boy's shirt upon arrival on the *Kulap Kanya,* but he had held onto the soft woolen garment his mother had made for him the year before he left her. He pulled it out now and grimaced to find it so faded and poor, so Chhayan street-rat. Niwut, the Captain's servant, always dressed in silken robes and wore a neat velvet hat on his head, come rain or shine. He was the proper sort of person to serve a great man.

But Sur Agung had given orders, orders that came directly from the Captain himself.

Does the Captain remember? Munny wondered again as he shrugged himself out of his sailor's garment and into the woolen wrap-shirt, which was itchy and rather too small. *Does he remember my face at the window? Will he speak of it? Will he . . . ? Will he . . . ?*

His head whirling with questions, Munny slipped out of his flopping brown shoes and decided to go barefoot instead. Hazardous on the *Kulap Kanya,* for sure, but more respectful in the presence of the Captain. He hastened back up the hatch, deftly slipping around and under other sailors coming and going. These ignored him for the most part or, when they saw who he was, drew back. He was tainted by association with the stowaway.

Munny stood at last before the door of the Captain's cabin,

afraid to knock, afraid to enter. He found it cracked open and decided to peer inside. Perhaps the Captain wasn't in. Perhaps he wouldn't be needed after all. Perhaps . . .

No such luck.

The Captain stood with his back to the door. Though the ship rocked and swayed, it seemed to do so around the Captain himself, rather than taking him along with its swellings. He stood firm, as though he were planted on rock. His arms were crossed, and his black hair hung loose down his back, not in its accustomed braid.

"*I've sailed with him two ten-cycles of years,*" the old man had told Munny. "*And while I have withered and bent under the ocean's harsh caress, the Captain never has.*"

A question slipped into Munny's mind, a question he had never before bothered to consider: *How old is the Captain?*

It was then that Munny's gaze was caught by a pair of compelling eyes.

They were round like Leonard's, round to let the devils in or out. Except Munny could never imagine devils lurking behind those eyes, for they were too sad and too strong. They were lighter than Leonard's as well, as was the face in which they were set. A woman's face, pale but ruddy-cheeked, with soft, almost childish features. A Westerner, and not a beautiful one save for those strange, strange eyes. She wore her hair in a black net set with jewels, but much of it escaped to curl around her face. Her clothing was unlike anything Munny had ever before seen, even in Capaneus City, which teemed with Westerner women wearing all sorts of odd fashions.

Most interesting of all was what she wore upon her left hand.

Munny took a step into the room, unconscious of doing so. He squinted, trying to see better around the tall form of the

Captain.

On her finger, the woman wore an opal ring that looked like the blossoming of a star. She was either pulling it off or just sliding it into place; it was difficult to discern which from the painting.

For that's what it was, Munny realized with some uncertain disappointment. A tall portrait set in a gold frame, rendered with little skill. But the subject itself transcended the artist's talents, her eyes, her face, and that beautiful ring . . . all filled with life and vitality and mysterious sorrow that not even an inept painter could suppress.

"I would have you clear my table, if you would be so kind. And close the door behind you."

Munny gasped, nearly choking on his own breath. For the Captain had not turned, not moved as much as a hair.

Hastily pulling the door shut, Munny stumbled across the cabin to the table, which was full of dishes from the Captain's morning meal; a better meal than Munny had enjoyed, and yet scarcely touched. No wonder Cook grew so fat if he enjoyed leftovers like these day after day!

Trying not to keep glancing back at the Captain and the portrait, Munny hastily stacked dishes onto the bamboo tray left for the purpose. His hands shook, and he feared he might drop something, almost as much as he feared the Captain would speak again. Perhaps he could perform his task and escape before—

"How is Leonard the Clown faring these days, Munny?"

Munny bit his tongue in surprise, and his mouth filled with pain. The Captain knew his name? How horrible! How wonderful! Munny felt his heart swell along with his throbbing tongue.

Speaking around the pain, he mumbled, "Well enough,

Captain."

"He learns the ways of the *Kulap Kanya* swiftly?"

"I think so. Swift as I ever did," Munny replied. His hand shook so much that he feared he would lose his hold on the delicate porcelain bowl it held. He quickly added his other hand and used both to place it on the tray.

"And what do you make of him yourself?"

Munny dared glance his captain's way and was relieved when his eyes still met only a stern and rigid back. "I'm not sure, Captain," he said. "I think he's afraid. But not of . . ."

"Not of the goddess?" the Captain finished for him. And with these words he turned upon Munny, his eyes so full of secrets it was nearly overwhelming. Munny froze, his fingers just touching but not daring to take up a small teapot of fragile work.

The Captain looked at him, studying his small frame up and down. "No," he said, "I believe you are right. Leonard the Clown does not fear Risafeth. I believe he is unaware of his near peril at her will, suffering as he does under a peril nearer still."

Munny made neither answer nor any move.

"We will bring him safely to Lunthea Maly, won't we, Munny?" the Captain said. But he did not speak as though he expected an answer, so again Munny offered none. "We will bring him safely to Lunthea Maly and there let him choose his own dark future."

"I hope—" Munny began.

But he was interrupted by a sudden commotion on deck. First a rising murmur of voices, then many shouts, inarticulate in cacophony. But a pounding at the cabin door accompanied Sur Agung's voice bellowing, "Captain, you'd best come see this!"

The Captain's eyes widened a moment and still did not break

gaze with Munny's. "We'll keep him safe," he repeated. Then he turned and was gone, leaving the door open.

Munny put down the pot he held and scurried after. The deck was alive with hands, even those who were off watch, crawling up from the hatches and crowding the rails on the port side. They parted way for the Captain to pass through, but when Munny tried to follow, they closed in again, blocking him as solidly as a brick wall.

"Look! Look!" Munny heard voices crying.

"It's a sign!"

"She's warning us!"

"It's a sign, I tell you!"

Fearing he knew not what, Munny ran for the center mast and climbed partway up, using the handholds and footholds with unconscious confidence. Soon he was high enough to see over the heads of the gathered crew, out into the blue waters of the ocean. And he saw them.

They were water birds. Big white albatrosses, smaller seagulls, heavy cormorants, even deep-throated pelicans and sleek, black-faced terns. These and many more, hundreds of them, none of which should be seen this far out to sea.

They were all dead. Floating in a great mass.

Munny clung to the mast, pressing his cheek against its wood. The shouts of the frightened sailors below faded away, drowned out by the desolation of that sight. Death, reeking death, a sad flotilla upon the waves.

"I've never seen anything like that."

Munny looked down to where Leonard clung to the mast just beneath him, staring wide-eyed out at the waves. "How could this have happened? Were they sick? Caught in a sudden gale? Are they tangled in fishing nets?"

There was no fear in his voice. Not like in the voices of the sailors. He did not understand. He did not realize. It wasn't his fault, Munny told himself.

But it was.

Sharks and shredding scavengers of the deep gathered. The *Kulap Kanya*, caught in a brisk wind, sailed on, leaving the death upon the water far behind.

Risafeth watched all from below and smiled her mirthless grin.

RED
VEILS

IN HIS DREAM THAT NIGHT Munny found his path barred by red veil upon red veil. He pushed these aside, and they tore as they fell, lying at his feet in scattered ruin, like the leaves of a dying tree. But he did not care about that. He knew only that he must somehow push on; he must find what waited on the other side.

Through the veils, he heard a voice he recognized all too clearly.

"*I warned you to have nothing to do with him. The Chhayan sea-dog! What business had you, Kitar-born, pure and proud, dancing with one such as he?*"

Munny grabbed at the next veil with more vehemence. He had heard this tirade and others like it from Uncle Mokhtar more times than he liked to count.

"*And what good did it bring you? A natural-born brat, a tainted bloodline!*"

"*He is the son of my husband.*"

This second voice was enough to bring Munny to a gasping halt. *Mother!* He grasped the next veil and tore at it, but it would not give. *Mother! Mother!* He must get through to her.

"*Husband? That sailor? Our father would not acknowledge him, and I, as new head of our House, will not recognize your so-called marriage either. He got you with child, and he abandoned you.*"

"*His ship went down. He would have come home else. He would have wanted to see his son.*"

"*You tell yourself that pretty story, sister. And tell it to the whelp if it brings you comfort. But in the meanwhile, it is you who are dying here in this slum, this stink-hole.*"

"*We ask nothing of you. You need not come again.*"

"*Believe me, I won't. I'll leave you to die before I accept a Chhayan sailor's boy into our father's house.*"

"*Then this is goodbye, Mokhtar. For I will not send my son away.*"

The red veil gave at last. It fell in sticking pieces, like a ruined spider's web, and clung to Munny's hands. But still there were more, too many of them, between him and that face he longed so much to see.

He heard her singing now, and her voice was tremulous, like brittle frost upon a leaf, and equally as lovely.

"*Where did the songbird go?*
Beyond the mountains of the sun,

Beyond the gardens of the moon.
Where did my good boy go?
Far beyond the western sea
Beyond the sea, beyond the sea . . . ."

No, Mother! Munny wanted to shout, to somehow make himself heard through those suffocating veils. *No, Mother! I'm coming to you! I'm coming soon!*

Shaking the sticky remnants from his fingers, he reached out and grabbed the biggest and heaviest of the veils yet. It broke and pulled away like living flesh. With a scream, he forced himself one step more, two steps.

He heard his mother cough. He heard the dry heaving and then rasping wet. He tore down the last veil.

All he saw was blood.

"Wake up, boy. Wake up!"

Munny sat up with a gasp and would have toppled right out of his swinging hammock had not Leonard stood beside him, steadying it. Munny could just discern the stowaway's strange face in the lantern light pouring faintly through the doorway. It was mostly cast in shadows, but his eyes were large, bright, and concerned.

"Are you all right?" Leonard asked. "You were moaning in your sleep."

Munny realized that if he could see the stowaway's face, it was likely the stowaway could see the tears staining his own cheeks. With an angry curse he pushed himself out of the hammock, landing barefoot on the side away from Leonard. Other sailors, trying to sleep before their next watch, growled at him in turn as he passed by. The old man was nowhere in sight.

Munny hastened out of the sleeping cabin and up a ladder, emerging at last into the nighttime coolness on deck. All was quiet and lonely at this hour with only the sailors at their watch, and even the ocean was docile.

But an air of apprehension pervaded all. No one had forgotten—or ever would forget—the sight of the dead birds. The poor broken bodies, which should have been winging their way through the sky.

Munny made his way to the casks of Milden's Vineyard and sat there, alone. He wept hot, pulsing tears, and each one made him angry. He had vowed not to weep, not after the Big Storm! Not until he reached Lunthea Maly and found out for sure. So he dashed his hand across his face and snuffled loudly.

"I have pretty bad nightmares myself."

Munny startled as Leonard took a seat cross-legged beside him, pretending not to see his tears.

"Go away!" Munny growled.

But of course Leonard didn't know what he said. He merely nodded and leaned back against a cask. "I dream of home often. But it's not the home I like to remember. It's always smoke-covered. Ash-covered." He shuddered.

"I'm not crying!" Munny said. "And I don't want you here!"

"I dream of my family now and then," Leonard continued. "It's more than a year now since I saw any of them. I don't even know if they're alive. Those are bad dreams, because I cannot always see their faces. Maybe I don't even want to anymore."

"I'm not a baby! I don't need anybody!"

Leonard continued to talk on in his foreign jabber, gazing out at the sky and the waves and not looking at Munny. At last he seemed to come to an end and sat in silence.

Munny stared at his hands, which lay limp in his lap.

Then he said softly, "I think she'll be dead when I get home. I hope she went to my uncle's house when she found me gone. But she was so sick when I ran away."

Leonard looked at him then, and while there was no understanding in his eyes, there was deep compassion illuminated by the thin sliver of moon above.

"My father sailed away before I was born," Munny said. "She always wondered why he never returned. Now she'll wonder about me."

Leonard's brow wrinkled, as though he was trying very hard to make sense of the strange words. He placed a friendly hand on Munny's shoulder, but Munny shrugged it off brusquely. "Sorry," Leonard said, and put both hands on his knees. "Well, little Mooney, my friend," he said, struggling with the boy's name, which he found difficult to say, "We've only one choice. We must either cry at our troubles . . . or laugh."

With that, the devil-addled fool crossed his eyes, puffed out his cheeks, and used his thumbs to make his ears stand out. This was so startling to Munny that he stared opened-mouthed for a moment. Then he burst out laughing. "There," said Leonard, letting his face fall back into normal lines. "That did the trick."

"You're a monkey!" Munny cried. "A big, ugly monkey!"

Leonard laughed as well. Then he made the face again. Munny, still laughing, tried to copy him, but his eyes hurt, and he could not do it right. So instead he began to make squeaking

sounds like the monkeys he had heard at the fair upon occasion.

Leonard mimicked these noises, adding yet another level of hilarity to his expression. "Monkey!" Munny cried.

Leonard licked his lips. Then grimacing a little, he attempted the word himself. "Mon—key?"

But he could not manage the pronunciation. Instead of the Chhayan word for "monkey," he succeeded in saying "saucepan." This sent Munny into another fit of giggles. Encouraged, Leonard smiled hugely and said, "Saucepan! Saucepan! Saucepan! Oooo, oooo, eeeeeek!"

He puffed out his cheeks and scratched himself, and Munny laughed until his sides ached. Their world, however briefly, became one full of mirth where sorrows and hardship could not penetrate.

But then, the *Kulap Kanya* tilted.

Just as it had that time when they climbed to the lookout and the whole ship moved against the gentle pulse of the ocean; again, on this clear, calm night, the *Kulap Kanya* suddenly tilted so severely that men below were tossed from their hammocks, and Munny and Leonard fell over on their sides, grappling for a hold on the casks to steady themselves.

A wave rose up. Or not so much a wave as a column fountaining in an enormous plume of dark sea water and moonlight-touched foam. Munny looked up, and for half a moment—or perhaps half a lifetime—he thought he saw a face in that water.

A woman's face. An angry face.

Then the ocean slapped down hard upon the *Kulap Kanya*. Munny lost his grip on the cask and felt himself tumbling across the deck. He could not think, but the terror of being washed out to sea filled him without thought. He flailed his hands, his feet, seeking some purchase, some hold.

He struck the aft railing with his shoulder, and his scrawny limbs wrapped around it with such force that surely a hurricane could not have pulled him from it.

The wave swept across the ship, passing to the other side and on.

The ocean leveled out. The *Kulap Kanya* stood tall once more.

Munny, clutching the rail, found Leonard beside him, similarly attached, terror leaping in his eyes. "What was that?" the stowaway cried.

Bells rang, and sailors stormed the deck. From somewhere amid the din, Munny heard the Captain's voice rising above all others. "Silence! Silence, men of Noorhitam! Are you all such frightened kittens, here on your own sea?"

Then he called up to the lookout swiftly descending the mast, "What news, Uka? What did you see?"

But the poor sailor, falling at last upon the deck, could only gasp, "Risafeth! Risafeth! She demands her tithe!"

Only later did Munny learn that all the casks of Milden's Vineyard had been washed away, never to be recovered.

THE
UNICORN

B EST STAY CLOSE TO BOY AND ME," the old man told
Leonard that night. "Don't go alone. Never."

Munny and Leonard followed the old man down the hatch to wrap up in rough blankets, trying to drive away the chill of the water that had so nearly overwhelmed them. Once more Munny was painfully aware of the silent wall between him and the other sailors. He felt their gazes, felt the fear pulsing through the *Kulap Kanya* like the thud of his own heart.

He shivered in his blanket. The face of the woman in the water was clear in his memory: a beautiful face, a wild face. A face without mercy.

Risafeth. The Vengeful One.

Munny shivered uncontrollably. But it wasn't fear for his own life that shook him to the bones. He looked sideways up at the brown foreigner, likewise shivering, his face full of ignorance, unaware of everything, unaware of his danger.

If he is not given over, I will never see Lunthea Maly. I will never give Mother the white peonies.

In the darkness of the sailors' sleeping cabin, Munny sat on the rolling floor beneath his hammock, Leonard on one side, the old man on the other. And he felt as though Death himself surrounded him in suffocating embrace. There could be no good end to this. There could be no good choice, no right choice.

Risafeth the Vengeful ruled this ocean.

"Sleep now," the old man said, helping Munny up into his hammock. "Our watch begins soon, and we will work, and we will guard that with which we have been entrusted." He addressed himself to Leonard and spoke in Westerner. "Sleep, Fool."

So they climbed into their beds and lay sleepless until the bell called them for their watch. When at last they rose and returned to the world above deck, they found the sea becalmed.

Until that day, the *Kulap Kanya* had enjoyed fair breezes and swift progress out of Chiara Bay, as if Risafeth were willing to overlook all disobedience and speed their journey onward. The goddess was no longer feeling so lenient.

Surrounding the ship was a dead sea. All was unnaturally still. The battened sails strained against empty sky to catch even the faintest breath of wind, but there was none to be caught. Munny, standing under the silent sky, felt sick to his stomach. It took him a moment to realize why: The ship did not roll on the waves.

Staggering uncertainly, as though he had returned to land,

Munny made his way to the rails and looked over the side. He gasped at what he saw, and his knees buckled, nearly betraying him.

For the sea was completely still. Flat without the faintest ripple of tide or current, without even a hint of churning foam in the ship's wake. It had all turned to mirror glass, a perfect reflection of the clouds above, so that the poor boy felt dizzy, unable to tell up from down.

He sank to his knees, his face pressed between the railing bars. "Light of the Lordly Sun!" he prayed, but without focus, without meaning, purely in fear.

The old man took him by the shoulder. "Come back, Munny. Don't look at the sea. It will drive you mad if you gaze upon its face at this time."

Munny allowed himself to be pulled away. He could meet neither the old man's nor the stowaway's eyes but stood with his head bowed, his heart hammering in his throat. All he could hear was his mother's voice, lost and far away, whispering:

"Where did my good boy go?
Beyond the sea, beyond the sea . . . ."

For days on end, the world remained thus. The sky moved: the sun, the moon, the stars, and the few scattered clouds. But the world beneath the sky remained as though frozen. The sailors of the *Kulap Kanya* were like those lost out of their time, wandering in a slice of existence between realities. Madness lurked on the borders of each mind, waiting to devour any who wandered astray.

So they worked their daily tasks, they followed the routines tolled out by the ship's bells. They watched their water supply lower, their food supply dwindle. But they did not complain.

Instead they looked to the quarterdeck where Captain Sunan stood every day from sunup to sundown. He alone of all the crew dared stare into the face of that impenetrable sea. And if he was mad, he had been so for so long that no one knew the difference.

"You will see," the old man whispered to Munny again and again during those horrible days. "Captain will do the right thing. At the right time."

The whispers among the crew grew daily more bitter, more insistent. "He'll kill us all if he waits!" Chuo-tuk was heard saying. But Tu Bahurn cuffed him and told him to be silent.

The Captain had his reasons. The Captain must be trusted. Or all hope would be lost.

"You will see," the old man said. "In time, you will see."

But see what? Munny wondered. Would the Captain at long last go back on his word to the stowaway? Would he, when the last cask of fresh water ran dry, give in to the demands of the tithe and toss Leonard into that dead-calm sea? Did a promise matter if it was made to a devil-ridden foreigner?

"He can't. He can't do it!" Munny whispered to himself. He sat in the lookout on his hour of watch. This was the worst, the very worst place of all during that cursed time: up so close to the sun, with nothing but still, still ocean as far as his eyes could see. The haze of the Continent to the north was gone. It was all too easy for Munny to believe that there was no Continent anymore, no dry land, no home to which he would return.

It was all too easy to believe that Risafeth herself would

break the surface of the endless water and swallow them whole.

"But he can't do it," Munny whispered, blinking against the hugeness and the glare in his eyes. Below him, the sails were still and the riggers sat idly beside their lines, waiting for a wind, waiting for a task.

Waiting for a death.

"If the Captain gives in," Munny said to himself, clenching his small hands into fists, "I will fight. I will fight them all! We have come too far to give Lhe-nad up now."

He felt the madness of silence laughing at his futile protestations. His head was light, and a wretched pain stabbed behind his eyes. He sat with his back to the mast, and he might as well have been in his own bed back home, so quiet was the world around him. He tilted his face to the sky, closing his eyes, and tried once more to offer a prayer. "Light of the Lordly Sun," he whispered. "Light of the Lordly Sun."

When he opened his eyes again, he beheld a sight not meant for mortals.

He had heard tell of such creatures before, within the first few days of his service. The *Lauté Dara*, the Water Stars, they were called. The children of the moon who long ages ago had shot from the heavens and landed in the deeps of the sea. There they mistook the welcome warmth of the vast ocean for their heavenly home and lived and sang as small reflections of their celestial brethren above. They were beautiful; they were magical; they were a gift and blessing to any man who saw them.

Munny saw one now. He saw it because of the wake it caused, the first ripple upon that still ocean in days. At first he did not know what it was, for it was too far away. But it drifted closer, as though propelled to meet the *Kulap Kanya* where she was stranded beneath the sky.

Munny stood up and leaned over the lookout rail. He opened his mouth to cry out, but he had no voice. How could he speak when he looked upon that which should never be seen in the mortal world? Perhaps the ship was no longer in the mortal world but had been transported to some horrible Between, where the Dara themselves could live alongside mortals.

Live . . . and die.

For Munny now saw, as the form upon the water drew near, that its throat had been torn out.

What a thing of grace! What a thing of exquisite beauty! White, but more than white, with a hide like mother-of-pearl, catching and refracting a million colors. A long mane and a longer tail, spinning and twirling like silken scarves of softest, wildest foam. The neck, once so elegantly arched, now ripped and shredded. And the proud horn which had protruded from its brow, now broken.

Sailors gathered below. Munny did not need to call out to them, to tell them of what drifted past. They gathered of their own accord, as if summoned, and looked down in solemn horror to watch the sea unicorn float by and away. All of them knew what it was without being told. Had they not dreamed of it every night they had stood watch beneath the vast arch of heaven? Had they not all believed they heard the stars of the water singing back to the stars in the sky, and had the song not buoyed the spirits of even the most desperate, the most jaded man?

Even so did the sight of the dead unicorn cripple the hearts of those who looked upon it. After it passed the *Kulap Kanya*, they turned to watch it disappear over the horizon into a wall of brewing storm clouds.

The sight of those clouds brought Munny out of the trance into which he had fallen. A storm! A storm was coming! That meant wind and release from this chain-like calm. He should ring the bell, he should shout the alert.

But he could not bring himself to interrupt the heartbroken silence below. So instead, he swung himself over the rail and climbed down the mast, nimble as a squirrel. He could feel the tension of brewing anger in the sailors as he neared the deck, as a lobster must feel the nearing heat of boiling water.

Just as Munny's feet touched the wooden boards, the thread of the thin spell that had held the *Kulap Kanya* entranced suddenly snapped. And the first voice spoke:

"It's a curse! It's a curse upon us all!"

Others followed, bubbling up in a roiling tumult of fear and agitation.

"Risafeth's fury! Risafeth's wrath! Risafeth's vengeance!"

"We must give her what she asks!"

"The tithe!"

"The tithe!"

"The tithe!"

Munny elbowed and jostled his way through the throng, searching for the old man, searching for Leonard. He told himself he heard Leonard's strange voice rising up from among the others, and he made for that. Then suddenly he did hear Leonard, and he was shouting like a mad animal.

"*Oi!* What do you think you're doing? Put me down! I say, put me down!"

Chuo-tuk and another brawny sailor had caught the foreigner by his arms and hauled him from his feet. Munny had a fleeting glimpse of the stowaway being carried through the crowd toward the stern rail. Munny screamed ineffectually, his voice lost in the continued shouts of:

"The tithe!"

"The tithe!"

"The tithe!"

This was it then. This was the end of the clown, the devil-man. Even as the storm clouds built upon the horizon, the crew would cast him overboard and pray that Risafeth would be appeased.

"*Stop!*" Munny shouted.

At the same time a much louder voice seemed to fill the very sails themselves with its power.

"Stop."

The Captain stood above them on the quarterdeck, looking down upon the scene. He lifted one hand, its long finger pointed at Chuo-tuk and the other sailor, who had Leonard halfway over the rail. "Put him down," the Captain said.

Neither sailor dared to protest. They set their captive on his feet and backed away, blending into the crowd.

The Captain's silence weighed upon the *Kulap Kanya* with as much iron force as his gaze. He beckoned to Leonard, speaking then in Westerner, "Come to me, Leonard the Fool. Come to me while you still can."

Leonard wasted no time. The sailors parted to let him through, and he met the Captain on the quarterdeck stairs. "Go to my cabin," the Captain said. Even as he spoke, the first of the storm winds touched his face, blew strands of his long black hair out behind him. "Wait inside."

The stowaway obeyed, and the Captain turned to face his crew.

"I gave my word," he said. "When I gave my word, it was the word of the *Kulap Kanya*. You are all part of the *Kulap Kanya*. You are all part of my word."

"But the tithe!" cried out someone in the crowd, thinking himself safely anonymous.

The Captain, however, stepped through, pushing aside those who were not swift enough to leap from his path. He made straight for the voice of he who had spoken, none other than Sur Agung, the quartermaster.

"Do you doubt my word, Agung?" the Captain asked. "After all these years?"

"Please—" Sur Agung began.

The Captain put up one hand. "Come to my cabin. You will have your say, my old friend, but you will have it in private, and under the eyes of him you would condemn to death. Come, Agung, if you are willing."

Sur Agung hesitated. His face looked quite old in that moment, as old as Tu Pich's. But then he nodded and preceded his master to the cabin, under the silent, pleading gazes of the crew. All of them begged him with their eyes, "Convince him! Convince him and save us! Only you can convince him, Sur Agung!"

Munny felt another gust of wind on the back of his head. He turned and saw the wall of the oncoming storm.

CRADLE
HITCH

SCARCELY HAD THE DOOR OF THE CAPTAIN'S cabin clicked shut before Munny felt Chuo-tuk's fingers digging into the flesh of his shoulder. He knew, even before he turned his snarling face up to his nemesis and made a futile attempt to shake him off, exactly what Chuo-tuk and the others intended.

Saknu, at a nod from Tu Bahurn, stepped over and caught Munny by the other arm. "No!" Munny growled. "I won't do it! Not this time!" He writhed and kicked and would have bitten if he'd had the strength to pull their hands close enough to his mouth.

But they were big boys, made all the stronger by their fear. Saknu clamped a smelly hand down over Munny's mouth, stifling his protests, and they carried him up to the quarterdeck, where Tu Bahurn stood with a length of rope.

Munny cast about desperately but could not see the old man anywhere in the crowd. Not that Tu Pich could do anything in the face of Bahurn's stern terror.

Chuo-tuk and Saknu lifted Munny right off his feet for the last few paces then thumped him down hard before the boatswain. Bahurn was already twisting his rope into a knot Munny recognized. "You know what we need," Bahurn said.

Munny grimaced, showing his teeth like an angry puppy. But everyone was gathered near: the sailing master, the riggers, Cook, even Tu Niwut, the Captain's man-servant. Their eyes were hooded and dark, and not even the sailing master made a move to hinder Bahurn.

"I won't do it," Munny snarled.

"You will," Bahurn replied, and Munny's eyes watched the movement of his fingers. "You will, or I'll tie a different knot, this one for your neck."

Munny drew a deep breath. He almost dared Bahurn to do his worst, almost called his bluff.

But then he thought, *I must bring her the white peonies.*

"Dragon's teeth," he said, his small voice spitting out the words. "Give me the rope then."

Bahurn, much to Munny's surprise, handed the rope over without a murmur. Hastily Munny pulled apart Bahurn's work and began to retie it. For a moment he considered Pich's Knot . . . but no. He couldn't take the risk. But his Cradle Hitch, that was a lucky knot, wasn't it? It had saved Leonard's life. Any knot that saved a man—even a condemned man—was a lucky knot tied by lucky hands.

So Munny worked quickly, crossing and weaving until he'd formed a hitch around his small body. Leaving the extra length in Chuo-tuk's and Saknu's strong hands, he approached the rail once more, even as he had all those weeks ago when the devil-man was first dragged from the hold.

This time, however, he looked down into a sea of mirror-glass.

Munny had only ever seen a mirror once. It had been only a piece lying broken in the Chhayan alleys of Lunthea Maly. While making his way home from the harbor, where he spent his days running odd jobs for pennies, his attention had been caught by something so bright, so gleaming, he thought it must be a jewel. But when he stepped closer, it was not a jewel he saw but his own two eyes looking up at him from the ground.

He had startled and hurried on his way, telling his mother all about the strange object when he reached home. She had smiled over her stitching, her fingers never pausing in their work, and said with a laugh, "*You went looking for a jewel, but your eyes were the best and brightest jewels the mirror knew to show you!*"

Munny had thought this silly tosh and gone to sulk by the fire.

But he thought of his mother's words now as he climbed over the rail. His reflected self, so far down, mimicked his every move, even when he stuck out his tongue to prove that he was not scared. It looked foolish, even spiteful in the reflection, and Munny wished he could take it back.

The smooth surface looked hard as stone, and the sunlight bounced off it blindingly. It was a perfect cover for anything that might lurk below. Risafeth herself might glide just inches beneath the surface, and how would Munny ever know?

It was easier to walk down the hull as they lowered him than it had been that first time. The ship did not move even a hair's breadth but remained perfectly still. Munny clambered silently down, his hands clinging to the rope, his feet guiding his progress, and inched himself toward the window. It was shut this time; but with the air so silent all around, no wind, no murmur of waves, Munny had only to put his face near the glass to hear every word inside.

"What about your word to your men?" Sur Agung's voice held more agitation than Munny had ever heard in it before. "You vowed to protect all those under your command. Yet you put them all at risk for the sake of this stranger. This devil."

Munny carefully tilted his face until he could see with one eye into the room. It was difficult to discern much in the shadows, so bright was the glare of the sun upon the glassy water behind him. Sur Agung was nothing more than a dark form, and Munny could not see the Captain at all.

Instead his gaze fell upon Leonard sitting on the floor directly across the room, his back to the wall, his elbows resting on his knees. His head was bowed, so all Munny could see of his face was his puckered forehead. He could have no idea what was being said between Agung and the Captain, but by now he certainly must understand that his life was at stake.

"I forget nothing," the Captain said calmly. Though Munny could not see him, he easily envisioned the quiet lines of his face. "I remember my vows. And I will see the men safely to Lunthea Maly. All of them."

"How?" Sur Agung cried. "You know as well as I that we no longer sail the same sea. You saw the Lauté Dara . . . you saw what we know cannot exist, cannot be, cannot enter our own world. We might even now be dead men, lost in this hell! You might have already failed us."

"If that is so, I see no use in throwing the Fool overboard," Captain replied. "If we're in a hell, we're in it together. And we'll sail together to the end."

Sur Agung took a stormy pace backwards, blocking Munny's view of Leonard. Now he could see the Captain's narrow form, standing with his arms crossed. Behind him hung the gold-framed portrait Munny had glimpsed before. The light passing through the window glanced off the blade of an unsheathed knife lying on the Captain's desk and reflected up to illuminate the portrait's eyes. It seemed to Munny as though the strange-looking young woman gazed down upon the Captain. What she thought of him in that moment was anyone's guess.

"Risafeth will tear us apart," Sur Agung said. "She knows her rights. For centuries now we have paid her tithe, and none who failed to do so have been seen again."

"An untrustworthy report at best, you must admit," the Captain said, blinking slowly, like a cat not quite at doze, "if the only men who might verify the story were all lost."

"Some stories are true without witness," Agung said. "Risafeth is one such story. You know as well as I, my Captain. I've sailed with you these many years, and I know you feel the heartbeat of this ocean more deeply than any three men alive. You know the truth of Risafeth. You know the goddess will have her due. The only question is this: Will she take him alone, or the rest of us along with him?"

"None," the Captain replied. "I do not fear Risafeth."

"But we do, and we are not you!" Agung replied, and he took two paces nearer the Captain, his hands up imploringly. Once more Munny could see the stowaway. Leonard's head was up now, and he met Munny's gaze right through the window.

Leonard smiled. Though his brow remained furrowed, his mouth twisted into a lop-sided grin, and he winked broadly at Munny. Then he puffed out his cheeks and crossed his eyes.

Munny gasped and swung from the window, pressing a hand to his mouth. Up above him Chuo-tuk, Bahurn, and the others lined the railing, and he could hear them hissing commands down to him, though he could not discern the words. He felt a tug at the rope and knew they meant for him to climb up and tell them what he had managed to hear.

He grasped the rope and tugged back, bracing his feet on the hull. He took a step, pulled . . .

And the Cradle Hitch—his lucky knot—came undone around him.

For an instant he hung suspended. But his grip on the rope was not strong enough, and all his weight had been in the hitch itself. He felt that horrible moment of near weightlessness just before the pull of gravity clutched him in inevitable claws.

With a thin cry, he fell.

The ocean shattered into fragments of light and glass and water as he penetrated the surface, and darkness swept over his head.

BREWING STORM

COLD WRAPPED AROUND HIM, cold and gloom that felt strangely welcoming after the heat and the glare of the sun on the water above. Down below, the sun could not penetrate. Down below, all was calm, all was still. All was over.

But Munny was not a boy to give up easily.

Though his whole body wanted to freeze with shock and terror, his heart surged, insisting he move, insisting he act. So, though he did not wish to, he forced himself to open his eyes.

He could see clearly down in the water, more clearly even than he could see above. This was almost the worst terror of all, almost enough to stop his surging heart.

For surrounding him in the dark were bright eyes.

Some were beautiful. Some were ugly. Some were enormous globes full of frozen dread. Some were small, like little lanterns, and gentle. But all watched him from a safe distance, curious, gathered beneath the hull of the *Kulap Kanya*.

Munny nearly opened his mouth to scream. But instead a thought flashed across his mind, driving him to action, driving him to move his arms, to struggle for the distant surface:

White peonies.

Above him the sun stabbed spears of light through the darkness, like arms reaching down to him. Munny fought to grasp them, forgetting the few swimming lessons he'd had, forgetting how to shape himself into a fish, to use his hands like fins. He clawed instead, as though he could tear away the resisting water as he had torn away the red veils of his nightmare. But he felt the endless darkness below stretch up and up to grab his ankles, to wrap around his knees, to pull him down into forever.

The light on the surface broke.

With a rush of white bubbles, something sank down beside Munny. And when the bubbles cleared, Munny saw the stowaway blinking and turning his head here and there, his arms moving uncertainly around him.

So they've given him up to Risafeth at last, Munny thought without really thinking, for real thoughts could not form in the shadows of this ocean. *They've given him up, and now we're both lost.*

But Leonard, realizing as quickly as Munny had that he could see clearly even underwater, turned sharply, his hair sweeping back from his face. He saw Munny, and his eyes widened in surprise.

He wasted no time, however, but shot out an arm and grabbed

the boy. Only then did Munny realize that the clown held a rope in his other hand.

Kicking like mad men, they shot for the surface, and the many hundreds of eyes watched them go without protest. They broke through with the tinkling shatter of glass, and shards of glass left cuts on Munny's face and arms. But he clung to Leonard, who in turn clung to the rope. Distantly, Munny thought he heard shouts, and then more ropes were tossed down.

"Here, tie this around you," Leonard gasped. Munny did not understand, but his hands worked of their own accord, and he made a simple hitch that would scarcely hold a pound of flour. It did not matter, though, for his fists gripped like death, and he and the stowaway were soon pulled up from the water, using their feet to navigate the hull.

Then they lay coughing, sputtering, and dripping water and pieces of glass upon the deck.

"He did it! He did it!" were the first words Munny understood through the rattling drums that pounded in his brain. "The devil found him!"

Suddenly, strong skinny arms were around Munny, and he was pulled up onto his knees to lean, still coughing, against a thin chest. "My boy! My boy!" wheezed a voice Munny did not at first recognize. For Tu Pich was too old to feel emotion; Tu Pich was too old to care or to cry.

Munny could not think of that now. His mind whirled with a question that could not quite take coherent form but which left him dizzy and gasping.

Why did she not take him? Why did she let us go?

The commotion of voices all around, even the voice that could not be the old man's, silenced suddenly as the shadow of the

Captain fell across them. Munny, blinking and wiping water and blood from his eyes, looked up and saw the crowd parting to let the Captain through. He was tall and seemed as otherworldly as anything on this strange sea, with the sun shining behind him. Munny could not see his face.

"Well done, Leonard the Fool," the Captain said, addressing himself in Westerner to the stowaway, who sat near to Munny, shaking himself out and trying ineffectually to wring water from his ears. "Your foolishness has proven worthy this time. We thank you for a life restored."

Leonard shrugged, but his face was sharp as he glared up at the Captain. "Why did no one else go after him? Were they going to leave him to drown? Why did you give no orders?"

Munny heard accusation in Leonard's tone, and he shuddered, wondering how the Captain would respond. But the Captain merely inclined his head slightly, and his voice did not alter as he responded, still in Westerner, "This was your task and yours alone. And it may yet prove your own salvation."

Leonard's brow wrinkled in confusion and frustration. But before he could speak again, the whole of the *Kulap Kanya* groaned and shifted suddenly under a sharp gale. All eyes on deck turned and saw the once-distant storm clouds suddenly bearing down upon them. Munny believed he saw roiling faces in those clouds, angry faces like gods ready to mete out judgment and retribution.

"She is coming," Captain Sunan said, gazing along with the others into the oncoming wrath. He whirled upon Leonard suddenly and hauled him to his feet, proving the great strength of his arm. "Get down into the hold," he said. "Do not return to the deck unless Munny or I come for you. Go!"

Leonard, staggering and casting terrified looks back over his shoulder at the storm, hastened for the hatch, and the sailors backed away and did not impede his progress. They were like dead men, their faces pale and lifeless in the shadow of what approached.

"Riggers, to the tack lines!" Captain Sunan barked. "Reef the sails and head to wind!"

RISAFETH VENGEFUL

THE DRIVING SHEET OF RAIN struck the glassy sea, and the glass shattered under its force, breaking into knife-capped waves. The eerie peace which had imprisoned the *Kulap Kanya* for weeks vanished in a moment, giving way to the animal fury of sea and sky and power greater than both.

The ship groaned again and surged beneath Munny's feet. Then rain pounded the deck and battered the sailors, powerful enough to knock many of them, even the brawniest, to their knees. Munny was flattened; and he shut his eyes, his arms over his head, and screamed inarticulately.

A hand landed on his shoulder, pulled him upright. Munny clenched his teeth against his screams and looked up into the old man's face, at the lines and crevices of his cheeks etched with water, like so many canyon rivers.

"To the tack line!" the old man shouted, and his voice could scarcely be heard above the rain and the roaring wind that attacked the battened sails above. Slipping and sliding, Munny scrambled after the old man who, despite his age, sprang with unexpected agility up the forecastle stairs to the forward mast where the riggers struggled to secure the tack line and reef the sail.

Though his small arms could scarcely add to the pull of the struggling sailors, Munny flung himself at the line and hauled with all his might to the rhythm of Odi the rigger's bellowed commands. The sail shrieked and groaned, torn by the gale and rain, and Munny wondered that the Captain had not given orders to lower all sails entirely.

The helmsman and four sailors at the wheel were hardly enough to pull the rudder in line against the beating waves. They clung to the spokes, their feet slipping across the deck, in imminent peril of the wind tearing them off into the hurtling sea. Even as the riggers followed the Captain's command and reefed the sails into position, the *Kulap Kanya* refused to head to wind. Any moment, she would capsize.

The Captain himself, his voice weirdly calm though it carried above the angriest roar of the wind, said, "Give it to me!" He took the helm, and by his own strength he did what five men could not. He turned the wheel, and the chains groaned and ground below the deck. The rudder shifted, and the ship turned into the wind so that the reefed sails were spared at the last, and the *Kulap Kanya* leveled out.

The ocean bucked and churned. The sturdy vessel plunged down into deep troughs of dark sea. Munny lost his balance and fell, and only his death-grip on the tack line prevented him from sliding across the forecastle deck. Someone grabbed him from behind and put him back on his feet. He braced himself and pulled, pulled, pulled to keep the sail in place, to keep the line secure. The Big Storm had been nothing to this. It had been a spring shower, a slight disturbance. No storm Munny ever could face again would be the equal of this, with the snarling faces in the clouds above spitting their rage and their lightning down upon the tormented ocean.

"We're going to die!" screamed a voice that carried back to Munny's ears. Chuo-tuk, hauling the line just in front of Munny, turned suddenly, gazing back over his shoulder, his eyes blinking against the rain, his mouth open and gasping for each breath.

"Pull!" shouted the old man, and Odi's bellow echoed him. "Pull!"

But Chuo-tuk cried, "She must have her tithe!"

He dropped the line and, falling to his hands and knees, scrambled across the deck, slipping and sliding, making for the forecastle hatch.

"Chuo-tuk! Get back!" Tu Bahurn yelled from the darkness.

But Chuo-tuk's gaze was fixed on the hatch. He muttered and babbled, only one real word spilling from his mouth. "Tithe! The tithe!"

Just as his hands grasped the hatch, the Captain's foot came down hard. Though the wind and the waves tossed the *Kulap Kanya* like a toy craft of sticks and leaves, the Captain stood firm, his body swaying with each heave, his heart beating in time with the ocean, with the ship, with the sky. He had left the wheel in the hands of the five straining sailors and walked across the shifting deck of his vessel to stand now above the addled Chuo-tuk.

He carried a drawn sword in his hand.

"Back to your station," he said, and all those on the forecastle deck heard him, even those who struggled to discern Odi's cries.

Chuo-tuk stared up at his master then backed away on his hands and knees, scrabbling for purchase on the deck. "The tithe!" he shrieked again. "She must have it!"

"To your station!" the Captain repeated; and Chuo-tuk obeyed, though tears may have wetted his face along with the pouring rain. The Captain remained at the hatch, leaving the wheel to the helmsman and his four sailors, who lashed it in place and struggled amongst them to keep the ship on course into the wind. Several of the men cast looks back to the hatch, their thoughts mirroring Chuo-tuk's. But the Captain remained where he stood.

Though no one could hear him say it, he ground through clenched teeth, "She'll take none of mine this night. She'll take none against his will!"

The ocean opened.

Like a pit into the very deeps of blackest anguish it opened, and out from that opening rose a face and a form such as had never been seen in mortal seas. A sinewy body, a neck glistening in the rain like a million jewels captured from the treasure chests of a thousand drowned vessels. And eyes like dead moons. Full of wrath. Full of vengeance.

So Risafeth came at last.

PICH'S KNOT

P ULL!"
The old man's voice tore at Munny's ear, and his young limbs obeyed automatically. But his eyes, and the eyes of all those on the forecastle deck, were turned from their work and fixed upon that sight which they had all seen in their nightmares, in their most fevered dreams.

She was crowned in lightning, and lightning flashed from her mouth and her eyes. The ocean was her gown, and it poured from her in dark streams, like flowing hair.

She was a woman.

She was a serpent.

She was the goddess of vengeance, and she gnashed her great teeth.

Give me what is mine!

Her voice was like the ocean itself, battering the hull of the ship; like the rain shredding the shoulders and arms of the sailors; like the glass of the unreal sea breaking. Thunder roared with each word, and green fire threatened to set the sails ablaze.

The men of the *Kulap Kanya* screamed. Many dropped their tack lines and fell upon their knees, upon their faces, groveling and worshiping in terror that was repugnant to behold. Only the bravest held fast at their posts, and even they found their muscles so numbed with fear that they could scarcely keep the sails reefed, scarcely keep the rudder true.

But Captain Sunan strode across his heaving deck and put up a hand to ward off the rain and the wind so that he could gaze unblinking at she who towered above him.

"Risafeth!" he cried. "Return to your deeps! You have nothing to gain here!"

She sank down and down, and white foam swallowed her great head. But she rose again, nearer now, and the rolling mountains of her tail lashed all too near.

My tithe! Give me my tithe!

Munny let go of the line and fell to his knees. But the old man caught him by the back of his shirt and refused to let him fall to his face. With strength unexpected in his aged limbs, he hauled the boy back upright. "Pull!" he shouted. And it was his voice now, not Odi's, urging the riggers. "Pull! Pull!"

Risafeth undulated through the water, and her bulk tilted the ship. The masts groaned in agony.

Captain Sunan, his sword still drawn, shook the blade at her.

"You know who I am," he shouted. "You know what once I was. I do not fear you or any of your kind. Wanton and capricious fey, you will not force your laws upon me!"

Her head rose again, and this time the long neck stretched even above the highest mast and would have been lost in the darkness above, well beyond the few struggling lanterns of the ship. But her eyes flashed, and fire fell from her mouth and boiled the sea around her.

Dragon spawn!

The words fell from the mouth of a woman, but when she gnashed her teeth again, they were the fangs of a serpent.

I will take what I want, here in my own sea!

She roared, and her breath was a wind of hurricane force that ripped into the *Kulap Kanya* without mercy or remorse. Everyone heard the tear, the groan. Then the screams of the main mast riggers, both those who still held their tack line and those who had fallen away. Their voices were too addled, too desperate to be understood through the shriek of the storm, the pound of Risafeth's voice.

But Tu Bahurn shouted near to hand, and Munny understood him.

"The batten parrels! They're breaking!"

The sturdy lines that secured the sails to the main mast were tearing apart, their knots giving way. No matter how the brave riggers pulled, the sail flew wild, ripping out of their hold. Only a few parrels held true, and these were scarcely enough to keep the enormous mainsail reefed. If any more gave way, the sail would whip around and receive the full blast of the wind.

And the *Kulap Kanya* would surely capsize.

"Saknu! Chuo-tuk!" Tu Bahurn roared, turning to the

boatswain boys. "Get down there and climb aloft! Secure those parrels!"

But Saknu clung to his tack line as though he held onto the last thread of his own life. And Chuo-tuk sank to his knees, screaming, "I'll die! I'll die!"

"Dragons take you," Tu Bahurn cursed. "I'll do it myself!"

He swung himself down the forecastle stairs, rolling with the pitch of the sea. A wave washed over the deck and nearly knocked him from his feet, but he braced himself and achieved the main mast. The riggers screamed, and even those who had fallen away crawled to retrieve their holds on the tack line. But it was useless with the batten parrels flapping above and the sail tearing under the heavy rain and the shrieking wind.

Tu Bahurn wrapped his arms around the mast and sought for the handholds and footholds. But he was so big, and the grips were so small. Without a securing line, he climbed only a yard before the ship rolled and he fell to the deck. He landed with a crunch and a curse. Another wave scoured the deck, and if not for the quick arms of the nearest riggers, the boatswain would have been carried into the black ocean.

Munny watched from the forecastle deck.

"Pull! *Pull!*" the voice of the old man echoed in his mind.

Give me my tithe! the voice of Risafeth roared through his heart.

But he thought suddenly, *White peonies.*

The next moment he was springing down from the forecastle himself, slipping and sliding across the rolling deck until he had achieved the main mast. He took hold with his hands and feet and climbed, allowing his small body to sway with the hurtling ship. The wind tore at him, but he gripped hard, making certain of each new hand and foothold before he released the last.

So he scaled up to the sail and the first of the broken parrels. With one arm wrapped around the mast, he reached out with the other and caught at the flapping rope's end. He pulled it near, clutching it with fingers and teeth. The first knot he tried, the Knife Lanyard, was not strong enough and slipped free almost immediately.

Munny reached out, even as the *Kulap Kanya* tossed on the tormented sea. From the corner of his eye he saw the rising swell of Risafeth's tail, a mountain of shining scales laced in white foam. The wave of its rising sent the ship groaning nearly to its side. Munny wrapped both arms tight around the mast to keep from being lost into the ocean.

The sail flapped hard against him, like an enormous slapping hand. One of the battens struck him in the leg, and he thought he felt the bone crack. But he held firm, and when the ship righted itself, he reached once more for the loose parrel. He caught it and this time secured it with a different knot: the Mother's Arms.

It held.

I will not die here, he thought. *I must give her the white peonies.*

He climbed on up the mast. The next parrel was easier to catch, and he tied it too with the Mother's Arms. He climbed again, and the higher he went, the harder the wind blew and the more difficult was his hold.

Risafeth turned her massive head. Her eyes, full of the deepest white fires of the unreachable ocean floor, fixed upon the boy. She saw what he attempted.

She laughed.

The sound shot into Munny like arrows, and he screamed at

the pain of it. Only a few more parrels, and the sail would be secure. But he could not climb, could not move. He felt his arms willing to let go, his muscles trembling, ready to fail him. **Give it up! Give it up!** Risafeth's laughter seemed to say. **Give it up and die!**

"I won't," Munny gasped.

But his hands slipped.

A fist like granite caught him by the shoulder of his shirt and hauled him back against the mast. Though the ship tossed against the buffeting waves, strong arms held Munny in place. He felt a rope slide around his thin body, a securing line.

"No fear, my boy," a voice spoke into his ear. "Pich's Knot has never given way. Not when tied by Pich himself."

Though the rain stung his eyes, Munny turned and looked into the face of the old man beside him. Lightning seared the sky but reflected like gleaming stars in the depths of those dark eyes.

"Tie the parrels," the old man said. "Secure the sail."

Then he was climbing up above Munny, scrambling to the very top of the mast. Loose ropes lashed him like whips, and the flailing sail slapped at his legs. But he climbed until he achieved the lookout and pulled himself in.

There he stood, wrinkled and swaying, clinging to the lookout rail. He shouted, his voice thin and inaudible in the cacophony of the hurricane's violence.

But Risafeth turned. Her eyes widened at the sight of him. And she shuddered when she alone heard his words.

"I'll be your tithe, Risafeth," the old man said.

With that, he leapt from the lookout and plunged down and down, through the tearing rain, and vanished into the raging sea.

GODDESS FLED

IF THE STORM WAS A NIGHTMARE, more terrible by far was the sudden event of calm. Not the calm of the glassy, unreal sea, but the calm of a brisk day under a cloud-scattered sky, with a crisp but gentle wind filling the torn sails of the *Kulap Kanya.*

The ship lurched once then settled with a great splash into the ocean it well knew. A mortal ocean, part of the mortal world, where the water ran liquid, and the salt waves were full of death and birth, and currents mapped by sailors of old carved the paths of the deep.

Risafeth was fled. In her flight, she had expelled the *Kulap Kanya* from her realm.

Captain Sunan, standing at the rail with his sword upraised, gazed out across his own sea. But it was another he saw in a distant place that was still all too near. More than once had he traveled to realms beyond his own; and he knew how close they always were, they and all the terrors they held.

He knew the laws of the fey folk, knew them better than many of the fey themselves.

Slowly Captain Sunan lowered his sword arm. His face sagged with sorrow, but his eyes remained bright. "So, Risafeth," he whispered. "So you run in the face of true courage."

Down below the main mast, Munny heard the voices of the riggers crying. Some wept in relief, but most babbled in dread, unable to believe their own eyes, convinced they must be dead or dreaming.

Munny clung to the mast. His face was still upward-tilted, gazing beyond the last few loose parrels to the empty lookout above. The empty lookout where, moments before, the old man had stood.

Where is he?

Munny tried to climb. At first he could not make his limbs obey. His leg ached where it had been struck by the batten. When at last his arms moved, they were so weak that he surely would have fallen to the deck below and met his end if not for the secure fastening of Pich's Knot about his frame. He felt the thrill in his gut of a fall that did not happen. Then he took hold and pulled himself up, tying the next loose parrel with shaking, rain-dripping fingers. Water from the storm poured down his face like tears, but he wiped it away and climbed on to the next parrel.

Someone below was calling his name. He ignored it. He must tie the parrels. He must obey Tu Pich, for the old man would always check his work.

Where is he? Where is he?

"Munny, you have fulfilled your task. Come down."

Munny clung to the mast, his forehead pressed against the Mother's Arms knot he had just secured. The sail was full; wind whistled through its gaping tears, but it was secure once more. The tack line could control it. They were safe.

But Munny gazed up again to the empty lookout.

"Where is he?"

"Come down now."

The Captain's face was suddenly before him. In all the months of his first voyage, Munny had never before seen the Captain scale the mast. But of course the Captain could do anything. The Captain could even save them from the goddess.

Only he'd not saved them all.

Munny blinked, his vision strangely blurred. "Where is Tu Pich?" he said.

"He is gone, Munny," the Captain said. "He gave himself to protect you. To protect the *Kulap Kanya.*"

"Risafeth . . . she took him?"

The Captain shook his head. "No. She could not take him. Not when he offered himself freely. She can only take a sacrifice of vengeance. The sacrifice Tu Pich offered was too dreadful to her, too awful for her understanding. He paid the tithe, but she did not take him. And she fled from his offering. Vengeance cannot abide the agony of grace."

Even as he spoke, the Captain put his hand on Munny's shoulder and gently urged the boy to descend. The babble of the sailors faded away into silence as they drew near. Munny's feet found the deck, but his knees gave way, and he sank down hard, unable to rise.

"Good boy. Brave boy!"

At first Munny could not recognize the voice that spoke. He sat numb under the glare of the sun even as Tu Bahurn struggled to undo the securing line.

"You have proven yourself a braver sailor than any of us," Tu Bahurn said, the words thick upon his tongue. "Munny Stout-heart. Dragons eat it. Can't make my fingers obey."

Indeed, though several tried, none could undo the old man's work. Pich's Knot would not give way until at last the Captain stepped forward and cut it loose.

Munny closed his eyes and felt the breath of sea air upon his cheeks and drying out the rain in his hair. Little pieces of glass fell and landed tinkling upon the deck, but these melted away, unable to hold onto existence here in the mortal world.

Neither could the memory of what had been seen so short a time ago. The dark image of Risafeth's face, the white lightning in her eyes, the storm . . . these skulked away into the recesses of each man's mind, there to lurk. There to wait for those darkest nights when a man must lie awake and face the truth of his heart alone. Then each one of them would recall with utter vividness that storm-tossed sea and his own sobbing cries.

But for now it faded. The riggers picked themselves up and secured the tack line. Others hastened to climb the masts and see to the damaged sails, while more hurried to check the soundness of the hull.

Still Munny remained kneeling, his hands limp in his lap. Captain Sunan stood over him, and they mourned together in silence even as the boatswain and the quartermaster shouted commands to the crew.

Then the Captain bent and touched Munny's head. "Come," he said, "let us fetch our Fool."

Munny followed the Captain down the hatch. The Captain took a lantern with him as they descended ladders into the deepest reaches of the ship. There, in the storeroom where the last crumbs of Beauclair blue-crust were wrapped and packed in barrels, they heard a thin voice singing with forced merriment, as though to reassure itself:

> *"I am a hearty sailor-ho!*
> *I sail the mighty seas.*
> *I reef the sails, I swab and row,*
> *I feast on withered peas.*
> *Oh rum-tum-tiddle-dee ho, ho,*
> *Rum-tum-tiddle-dee*—Oh, no."

This was followed by the familiar sound of retching.

The Captain opened the storeroom door and shined his lantern in upon the sickly green face of Leonard the clown. Leonard blinked at the sudden light and wiped his mouth unhappily before he offered something that was likely intended to be a grin.

"That was . . . some storm, eh? Did we all drown? Because if so, I never guessed that the afterlife would be so . . . so . . . Ugh, I can *smell* that blue-crust!"

White Peonies

THEY PUT INTO PORT FIRST AT AJA, then at Dong Min. They traded and made good profit. Artisans and shipwrights' lads climbed the rigging and repaired the sails, replacing broken battens and ruined lines. The *Kulap Kanya* sailed on through calm seas.

Risafeth did not hinder the vessel's passage.

Munny bent his back over the never-ending task of scrubbing the briny deck. Though his head and shoulders were bowed so that none could see, a small smile—so small, it might almost not have been—kept tugging at the corners of his mouth. He remembered what the old man had told him:

"A true sailor, he can travel the whole world. But as he approaches the seas of his own port, he will smell it. Long before the lookout gives the word, he will smell his home."

Munny could smell Lunthea Maly, the City of Fragrant Flowers. He could smell the funk of his own narrow street, the mass of too many bodies pressed into close quarters and living on top of each other in a conglomeration of sickness and frustration and despair. And love. Somehow, in the midst of everything, there was still love. Like a magic thread winding through the trampled mat of life.

The *Kulap Kanya* was nearing home at last. He would find out for sure and put his nightmares to rest.

A shadow fell across the deck where Munny worked. He glared up irritably and found Chuo-tuk standing over him. Munny flinched out of habit but with no real need. For ever since that night—that night of which no one spoke—Chuo-tuk could not look Munny in the eye.

His gaze fixed nervously upon the scrub brush in Munny's hand as he spoke. "Captain wants to see Lhe-nad," he said, struggling, as they all did, with the stowaway's name. Ever since that unmentioned night, no one called him the devil-man. But they continued to avoid contact with him if possible.

Munny nodded curtly, and Chuo-tuk hastened away. Leonard worked near to Munny, muttering to himself as he always did. His hair had grown shaggy over the last many weeks, and a beard sprouted in unruly tufts across his cheeks. But he still managed to grin and laugh, most often at himself, Munny suspected.

"Lhe-nad," Munny said, and when Leonard glanced his way, he pointed to the Captain's cabin. "Go," he said. "Captain Sunan. Go."

Leonard looked puzzled for a moment then shrugged and dropped his brush in his bucket. "Thanks, Moo-ney," he said, and rumpled Munny's hair as he stepped past, making his way a little unsteadily across the deck. Leonard would never make a true seaman. He could not find his legs.

Munny returned to his work, but within moments the smile was pulling at his mouth again. He wondered how soon the lookout would give the cry and sound the bells, announcing Lunthea Maly and the end of the long voyage. Any day . . . any minute . . .

Leonard eventually returned, saying nothing as he grabbed his bucket and continued his work. They did not try to speak, for over the weeks and months each had struggled with the other's language. So they remained silent but companionable, thinking their own thoughts.

But that night, when their duties were momentarily accomplished and neither could rest, they went together to the main deck and stood looking out upon the dark expanse of sea and the brighter expanse of sky where the Dara shone above.

Did they truly sing? Munny wondered, standing there beside the clown, straining his ears to hear something beyond the waves and the wind and the creak of the *Kulap Kanya.*

"*They sing of the promise given their mother. The promise that her lost children would return to her one day.*"

Suddenly Leonard spoke. "He doesn't want me to go. He doesn't want me to search for Ay-Ibunda."

Munny turned at the only word he understood: "Ay-Ibunda," the Hidden Temple. He shuddered at the name. He'd forgotten about the conversation overheard so long ago. Once more he wondered what this odd foreigner could possibly know about this darkest, most secret story, this myth of which Munny had heard only whispers.

"But I have to," Leonard said. "It's my only hope. I cannot return home without some help for my family. My people. I cannot fail them."

The heaviness in Leonard's voice was startling. Munny put out a hand and touched the clown-man's shoulder comfortingly. He knew what that heaviness meant, if nothing else. He said in response, "I hope to find my mother. And I will give her white peonies."

Leonard smiled sadly and returned Munny's gesture, touching a hand to the boy's small shoulder. "I'm sorry about the old man. I'm sure you miss him. I wouldn't have thought him one to be lost in a storm. But I suppose he would rather die at sea than on land. He was a good man. And you are a good man, Moo-ney."

So they turned again and faced the ocean. Eventually the sun rose, spreading crimson across the waves, and the lookout gave the cry: "Lunthea Maly! Lunthea Maly!"

The *Kulap Kanya* was come home.

Leonard stayed on board to help with the unloading of the cargo. Munny suspected that he was afraid to venture down into the city on his own, especially after his first morning glimpse of its sprawling, endless streets, alleys, shops, markets, palaces, and temples. To a Westerner, the vastness of Lunthea Maly, greatest city of the Noorhitam Empire, must seem like a labyrinth in which he would be swallowed up and never seen again.

But Munny longed to spring from the deck and run; run into those familiar streets, up the narrow alleys he knew so well, on to the finer streets where he believed—where he must believe—he would find what he sought.

They worked, however, most of that day, following Tu Bahurn's shouted commands as swiftly as they could. Sweat poured down their faces and arms, and their muscles quivered with exhaustion, and still they worked until the sun was cresting the apex of the sky.

Then Captain Sunan was beside them. Both Munny and Leonard stopped what they were doing and saluted.

"You must go now, Fool," the Captain spoke in Westerner. He pressed a purse into the clown's hand. "You have served well. You have earned both your passage and this to help you on your way into the city."

Leonard accepted the purse with a bow, but his brow furrowed uncertainly. "Captain," he said, "I have to ask . . . Did I . . ." He hesitated, swallowing hard. "Did I bring danger to you and your crew? Was it my fault that—"

"The men of the *Kulap Kanya* know the risks and the laws of the sea," Captain Sunan said. "They do not make them, and neither do you. Now go, Leonard the Lightning Tongue. Do what you have purposed in your heart. I pray that you will not live to regret it."

So Leonard bowed again, and the Captain bowed in return. Then Leonard turned to Munny and extended his hand in Westerner fashion. "Farewell, Moo-ney," he said. "Thank you for everything. Someday I'll write a song about you."

"Goodbye, Lhe-nad," Munny said, and shook the clown's hand.

With that, Leonard tucked his purse into his shirt, where he wore the strange clown's motley hidden beneath Tu Pich's old cast-offs. Then he sprang down the gangplank, ignoring the shouts and jeers of the sailors, some of whom wished him luck, some of whom wished him dead, some of whom spat at his back. Soon he was losing himself in the port crowds, his odd voice becoming lost in the chaos as he sang:

> *"Oh rum-tum-tiddle-dee ho, ho!*
> *Rum-tum-tiddle-dee ho!"*

Munny wondered if he would ever see the clown again.

"Now," said Captain Sunan, and the boy hastily turned back to his master and bowed. "You too have a purpose here in our city, do you not?"

Munny nodded. "I do, Captain."

"Will you leave the *Kulap Kanya* for good? Or will you sail with me again?"

Munny opened his mouth, but words would not come right away. He felt his heart torn inside, torn with unanswered questions. But then it seemed to come together, and he knew somehow what his answer must be.

"I will sail with you," he said.

"That is good," the Captain replied. He placed another purse in Munny's hand. "This is your pay for a good voyage. I will see you back on deck in three days' time."

The next moment Munny's feet were flying. He was down the gangplank in a flash, unheeding of Tu Bahurn's cries behind him. The Captain had given him permission, and he could not wait even a second longer.

His world tilted when he reached land, for his legs were no longer accustomed to stable ground. But he staggered on, ignoring the sickness in his stomach, thrilling at the sights so familiar and yet so strange. He remembered all this, every turn of the port, and yet it seemed as though he must be dreaming to be back here. After everything he had seen, after everything he had experienced, this world of his home was more unreal even than Risafeth's glassy ocean.

He turned up a certain street and came upon a market. There was the stall he knew he would find, abounding in fresh-cut flowers. Only here had Munny ever smelled the fragrance attributed to his home city. Only here could he dream that Lunthea Maly was the garden of delights for which it had been named.

Only here had he seen white peonies, his mother's favorite.

"Away, dirty rat!" the seller of flowers growled, shaking his fist at Munny's approach. "Don't touch my pretties with your smelly hands!"

But Munny fumbled with his purse, and a flash of bright coin brought the seller round. "Please," Munny gasped, hardly able to get the words out now that he was here. "Please, I need white peonies."

The seller took his coins and selected three of the biggest, frilliest blooms. Munny's hand trembled as he accepted them; he felt as though he were given clouds of perfumed lace.

He ran on then, holding the blooms as gently as he could, close to his heart. His feet turned up streets less familiar, away from the markets, away from the Chhayan alleys. For surely Mother would not be there.

Surely when she had discovered him gone, she would have agreed to Uncle Mokhtar's offer. She would return to the home of her birth.

"*I wore white peonies in my hair the night I met your father,*" she had told him once, long ago. "*He said I looked like a Faerie princess.*"

The Kitar streets were better swept, though the stench of lower Lunthea Maly still rose up to pollute the air of even the finest gardens. Munny had only ever come a handful of times to his uncle's house, and the last time, Uncle Mokhtar had refused to let him through the gate. But he knew the way. He had run it in his head, in his dreams, a thousand times.

He came to the gate, the peonies in his hands a little battered from his run, but still full, still beautiful. He rattled the lock and shouted, "Uncle Mokhtar! Uncle Mokhtar!"

One of Mokhtar's old servants appeared at the door of the house, and with him came two great, bounding dogs. They ran barking at the gate, showing their fangs, and their snarls drowned out the servant's voice even as he shouted, "Go away! Go away, Chhayan brat!"

But Munny had looked into the face of Risafeth. He ignored his uncle's guard dogs and rattled the gate still louder. "Uncle, it's me! Come out!"

At last his uncle appeared at the door, wrapped in a blue silk robe, his feet shod in silver-tasseled slippers. He called off the dogs, called off his old servant, and waddled down the path to the gate, his face twisting into an ever-deeper sneer as he drew near.

"So," he said. "The rat returns to its hole. Never thought to see you again, Munny; no more than we saw your father."

"Uncle Mokhtar," Munny said, one hand clutching the gate, the other holding the peonies. "Where is she? Is she here? Is she in your back garden?"

Mokhtar's mouth twisted, and his arms folded over his ample chest. "No," he said. "She would not return to her father's house. Even when you abandoned her, she refused my offer. She refused her own brother. She will not be laid to rest in the grounds of her family."

Munny's heart sank. "Where is she?"

"Down in that stink-hole where your father left her. Where you left her. Buried and dead."

Munny was running again before Mokhtar had reached the end of his sentence. He was mostly down the street when his uncle's final words caught up to him in an angry bellow:

"You are dead to us too, Chhayan-born! You are dead, do you hear me?"

Munny shielded the peonies as best he could as he plunged once more into the Chhayan quarter, dodging and ducking all the bodies and carts and piles of garbage. No tears sprang to his eyes, for he could not cry, not yet. Perhaps he would cry later. Perhaps he would never cry again.

The Chhayan alley-ghosts, as they were known, were buried in a ditch just beyond the city. There were no markers on their graves. They were lost and forgotten by all.

But Munny would not think of that. He snarled his way through crowds, ignoring the shouts, avoiding thieving hands, his bare feet slapping on the stones, each step an agony as though he ran on hot coals.

He saw it. A little door, half-fallen from its hinges. A doorway to nowhere. To nothing. To everything.

Munny reached it and fell, his shoulder against the doorpost, unable to enter, unable to push through and find what he feared beyond. He stood there, the peonies cradled to his heart which beat

to bursting in his breast.

Then he heard it: the wet, tortured cough.

His heart stopped.

She sat at the only window, using the dirty light that spilled through as she bent over her work. She embroidered delicate leaves and birds and flowers into garments of silk, which her employer would collect at the end of the evening, leaving pennies for her efforts. She covered her mouth with a handkerchief when she coughed, permitting not even a trace of blood to mar her artistry.

Her face was haggard and drawn. Long vanished was the bloom of the pretty Faerie princess who had danced with her Chhayan sailor in the moonlight.

She was the most beautiful woman in the world.

When the door creaked open, she looked up, blinking in her effort to see through the shadows. When she smiled, her whole face became sunlight.

"There you are," she said.

Munny flew across the little chamber, across the dirty floor. He collapsed into her arms, crushing the white peonies against her, and their perfume filled the room. She held him close, pressing him to her, whispering over and over again his name. Not Munny, the name by which he was called, but his true name, the name she had given him at his birth. He wept and held her as though he would never let go, and she rocked him.

Her trembling voice, weak from the cough, murmured gently in his ear:

> *"Go to sleep, go to sleep,*
> *My good boy, go to sleep.*

Where did the songbird go?
Beyond the mountains of the sun.
Beyond the gardens of the moon.
Where did my good boy go?
Far beyond the western sea,
Then home to me, then home to me."

A Note to the Reader

Goddess Tithe takes place within the context of my larger novel, *Veiled Rose*. If you would like to learn answers to some of the questions about Leonard the Jester—Who is he really? Why is he traveling to Lunthea Maly? What does he want with the Hidden Temple?—I urge you to pick up that novel.

About the Author

Anne Elisabeth Stengl makes her home in Raleigh, North Carolina, where she lives with her husband, Rohan, a kindle of kitties, and one long-suffering dog. When she's not writing, she enjoys Shakespeare, opera, and tea, and practices piano, painting, and pastry baking. She studied illustration at Grace College and English literature at Campbell University. She is the author of *Heartless, Veiled Rose, Moonblood, Starflower,* and *Dragonwitch. Heartless* and *Veiled Rose* have each been honored with a Christy Award, and *Starflower* was voted winner of the 2013 Clive Staples Award.

From the Acclaimed Winner of the 2012 Christy Award for Visionary Fiction

shadow hand

TALES OF GOLDSTONE WOOD

Coming Spring 2014

from BETHANY HOUSE
a division of Baker Publishing Group
www.bethanyhouse.com

ANNE ELISABETH STENGL

Coming Soon

AN ALL-NEW
TALE OF GOLDSTONE WOOD

golden daughter

Timeless fantasy that will keep you spellbound!

Don't Miss the Rest of the
TALES OF GOLDSTONE WOOD

To learn more about Anne Elisabeth Stengl and her books visit
AnneElisabethStengl.blogspot.com

As Princess Una comes of age, a foolish
decision leaves her vulnerable to an
enemy she thought was only a myth. What will
Una risk to save her kingdom—and her heart?

Heartless

When a terrifying evil lays siege to the land, the
unusual friendship between Leo and Rose Red
undergoes a deadly test. What began as a game will
now decide the fate of a kingdom.

Veiled Rose

With the Night of Moonblood fast approaching, a
prince embarks on a desperate quest to stop the
goblin king from unleashing an ancient evil. But
does he have the courage to save those he loves?

Moonblood

On a mission to save his ladylove from the Dragonwitch, Eanrin comes upon a mortal maid trapped in an enchanted sleep. One waking kiss later, he is caught up in an adventure beyond anything he ever dreamed.

Starflower

As a Death-House Gate opens into the mortal world, monsters and war threaten the North Country. Only one man can turn back this tide, but to do so he must face the realm of the Dragonwitch.

Dragonwitch

The above titles are published by BETHANY HOUSE,

a division of Baker Publishing Group
www.bethanyhouse.com

ROOGLEWOOD PRESS

Discover more exciting ROOGLEWOOD PRESS titles!

www.RooglewoodPress.com

Like us on Facebook

Find more information on *GODDESS TITHE* at

www.GoddessTitheNovel.blogspot.com